TEN AND ME

•

Johnny D. Boggs

AVALON BOOKS
NEW YORK

SECOND PRINTING

PRINTED IN THE UNITED STATES OF AMERICA
ON ACID-FREE PAPER
BY HADDON CRAFTSMEN, BLOOMSBURG, PENNSYLVANIA

For my own heroes:
Johnny Cash, Bobby Darin, and Emmylou Harris;
George Brett, Cale Yarborough, and Hank Aaron;
Jimmy Stewart, Jean Arthur, and Ward Bond;
Jack Schaefer, Dorothy M. Johnson, and Mark Twain;
Francis Marion, Annie Oakley, and Walter Cronkite;
and
Jack Smith, Lisa Smith, and Darrell Boggs.

Prologue

*S*unday, May 16, 1886
New Mexico Territory

The *Santa Fe New Mexican* sent a reporter to cover my—our—wedding. So did the newspapers from Dallas, New York, St. Louis and Chicago, even *Harper's Weekly: A Journal of Civilization.* The *Harper's* scribe brought along an artist who spent most of the morning doing a woodcut engraving of my betrothed for the magazine. I admit I was a tad jealous; that fellow got to see my bride in her wedding gown before me.

So the reporters sat around in the parlor, sipping my rye, smoking my cigars and asking me about our honeymoon plans ("We are going to New Orleans for a couple of weeks"), if I would be interested in becoming a lawman again ("No. I haven't worn a gun in years, and she likes it that way") and if there were any truth to the rumors going around the Plaza that I might seek a position on the bench ("That's the dumbest thing I've ever heard").

In the end, though, they wanted to know more about Tenedore Keough than they did about the new Mr. and Mrs. John "Jack" Lindsay Mackinnon. I figured as much. A few years have passed since Ten's death, but I reckon he's even more famous now than he was when he was alive—and he had quite a reputation back then. Robin K. Hunter's books for The Five Cent Wide Awake Library helped make Ten a living legend from New York to San Francisco, and other cheap novels followed, but I imagine Ten would have made his mark on the frontier without the help of those journalists—liars might be a better word.

Tenedore Keough did just about everything a body could in a relatively short life. Texas Ranger, outlaw, gambler, deputy marshal, sheepherder, hired killer.

Oh, and dentist.

He turned out to be good at just about everything he ever did—except dentistry. He was a tooth-puller back in Texas when we first met.

Chapter One

I stepped off the train in Dallas, having left a thirty-two-acre farm outside Florence, South Carolina, to my greedy creditors. In the South after the War, land-hungry carpetbaggers seemed as thick as pond scum in a drought. I held on as long as I could before declaring if they were that excited to own my miserable swamp land, then they could have it. So I carved out "G.T.T." on my front door and was "Gone To Texas."

That had been in '75. Three years later, I arrived in Dallas. You see, I seldom bought tickets. I would hop a freight from time to time, and get thrown off every now and then. I worked, helping out farmers in Alabama and Tennessee ... sweating on the Mississippi River docks in Vicksburg for eighteen months ... serving as an apprentice gunsmith in Louisiana. Tired of New Orleans, I bought a ticket to Dallas and rode into Texas in a Pullman sleeper. I thought somebody was shooting off fireworks, when I stepped onto the Houston and Texas Central platform that spring evening. That's how green

I was, a twenty-eight-year-old farm boy with only a few dollars to my name after splurging on a ticket by rail. I owned the clothes on my back, boots on my feet and hat on my head, plus a haversack stuffed with long johns and extra socks, a .36-caliber Spiller and Burr revolver that would practically bust your thumb just trying to cock the piece, and one miserable toothache. The noise came from a tough-looking lot standing in the middle of the street, firing pistols in the air and passing a bottle of amber liquor.

"What's that commotion?" a whiskey drummer asked a porter.

"They're a bunch of Yanks celebratin' Lee's surrender. It's the twelfth of April."

The drummer spit. "News must be a little slow in these parts," he said. "The War ended thirteen years ago."

I would have smiled at the joke, but my tooth hurt too much, so I took my belongings and walked through town, stopping only to buy a copy of the *Dallas Weekly Herald* to see if a body might find work in this town. Dallas was bustling. I watched a couple of boys put up a stucco-walled house, one of those made-to-order contraptions from Chicago, and debated if I should eat or find somebody who could fix my tooth. I entered a red-front building named The Trinity River Saloon instead.

Two whiskeys dwindled my financial state by a full dollar—I guess rent was steep in a town like Dallas so the Trinity had to overcharge for watered-down rotgut—but did little to help my aching tooth. I moved on outside, wandered down Main Street, past saloons, dance halls and one opium den until I reached the business district. A dentist had an office in a bank, but both were closed, so I turned left and walked several more blocks until I saw a shingle hanging above a shanty: T. Keough, D.D.S.

He was open, so I walked in. There was no wait.

Rather puny and pale, with thin lips and lifeless blue eyes, Dr. Keough directed me into a chair, and turned to wash his hands in a blue-enamel basin. That's when I saw the butt of a pocket pistol stuck in his back waist-band. I wondered how many Dallas dentists went around armed but kept my mouth shut—until Keough turned around and told me to open wide.

He stuck some kind of probe into my mouth and bounced it off my uppers and lowers, mumbling a "Where you from, mister?" I told him, as best I could with his torture device and bony fingers in my mouth, and he nodded. I don't know how he understood a word I said, but he did.

"I'm from South Carolina myself. Charleston. I left immediately after the War, though. Don't know how you managed to stay ten years with carpetbaggers every-where."

"Dallas don't seem a whole lot better," I managed to say and tried to tell him about the celebration I had wit-nessed earlier that day when his metal poker banged on my bum tooth.

I screamed.

"So that's the one," he commented easily. Keough pulled a pewter flask from his coat pocket, unscrewed the cap and offered me his whiskey. When I saw the pliers he planned to use, I drank greedily. Next, he jammed the device into my mouth and jammed his left forearm across my chest, pushing down until the chair almost toppled over. I figured I had five inches and forty pounds on the dentist, but he sure was feisty and strong. The pliers cracked my tooth as the dentist grunted and pulled. Me? I yelled, squirmed and tried to light a shuck out the door, but Keough had me pinned pretty good. He grunted and breathed heavily in my face, his eyes flaming with determination. Suddenly, he started heaving, withdrew the pliers with my tooth still relatively intact in my mouth, and moved to the wash basin, coughing painfully. I sat up, rubbed my sore jaw and looked as Keough turned around, holding a white handkerchief to his mouth. The coughing spell had subsided, but from the dim yellow light of the lantern, I saw specks of blood on Keough's lips and handkerchief.

I jumped out of the chair and screamed: "You're a consumptive!" With both hands, I wiped my face savagely where he had coughed and breathed. Keough returned the bloody rag to his pocket and withdrew his whiskey. I remembered drinking from the same flask. At first, I felt sick. Then my anger got the better of me. I cursed, and stomped my boots. Keough drained the flask and wiped his mouth with the back of his hand as I headed for the door.

"You owe me two dollars," he said in a rasping voice.

I turned, glaring, and informed him that he had not pulled my tooth and I had no intention of paying a doctor with consumption for coughing in my face. Keough drew his pocket revolver I had forgotten about.

"One way or the other, mister," he said icily, "you're paying me."

He lurched forward suddenly. For a moment, I thought he was running after me, but he stumbled, coughing horribly again, and dropped the revolver. I looked at the pathetic little man, sitting on the floor, his hands gripping the arm of the chair with his head bowed as he hacked, coughed and groaned. My right hand found the door-knob, but I didn't leave.

Back in Florence, when I was fourteen, I found myself serving in the Confederate States of America Army. A prisoner of war camp had been established there, and I was a guard. The miserable stockade in the pines held plenty of Yankees as 1864 dragged on into 1865. The Yanks there, many of them transferred from the death trap in Andersonville, Georgia, were mere skeletons, and we didn't help them except for the rice, cornmeal and a handful of peas we gave them each day. Pretty soon, all they got was cornmeal. Few of them ever tried to escape. Mostly, they just died.

You watch men like that, it affects you. Sometimes, I would give Yankees my biscuit or a piece of bacon. It seemed the Christian thing to do. By the end of the war, us guards weren't eating much ourselves. Food was scarce throughout the Carolinas; Sherman had seen to that. I felt helpless watching those poor soldiers succumb to smallpox, scurvy, dysentery, or just exhaustion. I couldn't do much for them, but I promised myself I wouldn't let the sick die needlessly again. Fourteen years later, the thought of those Yankees made me release my grip on the doorknob. I helped Dr. Keough into the chair and waited until the coughing spell passed.

"Can I get you anything?" I asked.

He shook his head. I tried to make conversation.

"What's the 'T' stand for, Doc?"

"Tenedore," he answered. "May I have your name?"

"John Lindsay Mackinnon, but most folks call me Jack."

"Jack." He sounded so weak I thought he would die. "You're the first patient I've had in weeks. Sorry I didn't get your tooth pulled." He tried to catch his breath, and a few minutes passed before he could talk again. "You come back tomorrow."

"No thanks, Doc." I felt bad about that, but the last thing I needed was consumption. I looked away, ashamed.

"It's all right, Jack. I understand. Sorry I pulled a gun on you."

I sighed. "You probably should get another line of work, Doc."

"Call me Ten."

I did. He smiled, suppressed another cough, and motioned weakly to the rolltop desk in a corner. "Top drawer," he said. "Left side." I walked across the room, opened the drawer and returned with a bottle of rye. He took a long pull and sighed. "I'll be all right, Jack Mackinnon," he said. "Am pleased to make the acquaintance of a fellow South Carolinian. Go on. Find another dentist to take care of that tooth."

Before I left, though, I put two dollars on the top of his desk. Two days later, when I walked down that same street, a sign advertised the office space for rent. Dr. Tenedore Keough had pulled out of Dallas. I didn't see him again for four months.

My toothache passed, without me ever seeing another dentist. Meanwhile, I found gainful employment putting up those Chicago buildings. You couldn't actually call what I did carpentry. Those shacks went up in three hours with nothing more than two men using screwdrivers. But I was good at it, and at night I found I was even better at something else.

Poker had been a way to pass time before, gambling with my fellow guards at the Florence prison camp or with friends in New Orleans. In Dallas, it was a way to make money. I had to face reality. I didn't want to stay here, but I needed Yankee greenbacks to take me places, and even though I slept in the wagon yard to save money, I wasn't earning much putting up those ready-made houses.

I took leave of Dallas shortly after winning more than three hundred dollars in one night. A fellow named Fulton Fyfe and I were the only ones still in a game of five-card stud, and the betting got out of hand. Fyfe had two kings, a jack and a seven showing. I had two kings, a queen and a nine. He raised. I raised. He raised again. So did I. Finally he raised and I called. Smiling, he turned over an ace. I never would bet that much on a pair, even with an ace kicker. I turned over a matching queen.

Fyfe took exception, stood up, cursing, and reached for a giant bowie knife. I whipped out my .36, cracked his head open with the barrel and collected my winnings as two gents hauled the unconscious loser to the back alley.

"You shouldn't have done that, Jack," one of the card players informed me.

"Well, I wasn't about to let him gut me like a catfish."

"Do you know who Fulton Fyfe is?"

"Nope."

"He's wanted for murder among other things."

My mouth went drier than a lime burner's hat. "Well, how come nobody's taking him to jail?"

"Because he isn't wanted in Dallas. And nobody wants Fulton, Fraser and Forbes after him."

"Who are they?"

"Fraser and Forbes are his brothers. They're also wanted, Jack, and those fellows are going to kill you."

Chapter Two

Jacksboro was a long, dusty ride by stagecoach from Fort Worth, but it suited me, Jack Mackinnon, professional gambler. I had hopped a train to Fort Worth after my run-in with Fulton Fyfe before deciding that the Panther City was a tad too close to Dallas and the Fyfe brothers. Some folks might have called me a coward for departing Dallas and Fort Worth, but I saw no reason anyone should die—me or some Fyfe—over a stupid disagreement at a card table. Fulton had been drunk, was a bad loser, and I simply defended my innards, which I wanted to keep. I hoped he would wake up and forget about it when he learned I had left town. So I found a gambling parlor in Jacksboro and waited for the citizens to leave some of their pay with me.

Smoke and noise filled Bagwell's Palace when I walked in for my regular game one hot August night. I certainly didn't look like a professional gambler. My duds were the same I had brought with me from New Orleans, tan canvas britches and a pullover cotton shirt.

My only purchase had been a gunbelt and holster for my .36. Before, I merely tucked the Spiller and Burr in my waistband or mule-ear pocket. I wasn't sure if the money had been well spent. Now, when seated, the revolver's hammer pinched my side.

Dottie Bagwell brought a drink over and said she had hired a new faro dealer. She promised to introduce me later. I glanced at the guy sitting across the room. He looked familiar, but I couldn't place him. Maybe it was the smoke. It didn't matter. Dottie went back to business, as did I.

I lost early, which I liked. Someone once told me you have to spend money to make money in business, and I figured the rule applied with cards. Whenever I won early, I usually wound up losing for the night, so I was happy to be down twenty dollars after a few hours. By midnight, I was up two hundred.

It was a friendly game, too. My opponents included a retired officer with the Eleventh Infantry, three town merchants and a foreman from one of the big ranches down on Lost Creek. No ruffians like Fulton Fyfe. Dealing stud, I had just paired up my king when I heard the voice.

"You're a dead man."

Standing before me was big-nosed Fulton Fyfe.

My friendly opponents immediately left the table for the bar or safer climes. The guy banging on the piano stopped, and Bagwell's Palace turned deathly quiet. Fyfe wore a pair of Army Colts tucked butt forward on his hips. He kept glancing to his left, toward the entrance to Dottie's storeroom. I leaned forward in my chair, but the Spiller and Burr's hammer dug uncomfortably into my side so I leaned back, quickly realizing that this position made it easier to draw my revolver anyway.

"Fyfe," Dottie said. *Good old Dottie,* I thought. She hailed from Georgia, so I had hoped she would stick up for a fellow Southerner, not taking into account that Texas was also part of the South. "Take this outside, you hear me? I don't want any gunplay in my house."

"Shut up," Fyfe said.

Dottie chewed her bottom lip angrily, cursed once and said, "All right, but get this over in a hurry. You're spoiling business."

I lost my respect for Dottie right then and there. I was no gunman, but I had to become one. Fyfe would kill me. Of this I was certain, so when his eyes darted toward the storeroom again, I made my play.

Pushing back the chair while drawing the Spiller and Burr, I stood and sent the chair crashing to the floor. "Fulton!" I shouted as the hammer cocked. Fyfe yelled something himself, stepped back and reached across his body for one of the Colts. The .36 boomed, and Fulton Fyfe disappeared in a cloud of thick, sickening smoke. I moved quickly to my right, heard the report of a pistol, felt the buzz of a bullet. I fired into the smoke, kept moving to the right, thumbed back the hammer again and crouched.

Someone screamed.

I heard the door bang open, realized what was happening and leaped forward, twisting in the air. My left shoulder hit the hardwood floor as the shotgun roared. Buckshot splintered the floor, but not me. I only had a glimpse of the gunman as he came through the storeroom, and he also vanished in a cloud of smoke from the shotgun he had just fired. The .36 bucked again. I cocked the gun and fired. A shot roared beside me, and fiery pain scorched my neck. I dropped to my back and rolled over, ripped back the hammer and saw Fulton Forbes.

He sat on the floor, trying to cock his Colt with both hands, blood pouring from two holes in his chest. The man was so close to me we could touch each other. My bandanna smoked. I realized the piece of cotton was on fire and slowly comprehended that Fulton Forbes had fired the last shot. How he missed, I don't know. We were at point-blank range. I pulled the trigger.

I rolled over, cocked the Spiller and Burr again and waited. Nothing happened. I sat up, quickly ripped off the smoking bandanna and tossed it onto the floor and struggled to my feet, coughing from the smoke. When the thick clouds drifted away, I saw the two men. First I looked at Fulton Fyfe, and almost vomited. When I could move, I walked across the saloon and stared at the other man. He was still alive, so I kicked the shotgun out of his reach, though that proved unnecessary. The would-be killer stared at me, muttered a curse and died. I could see the resemblance between him and Fulton.

I breathed again, holstered my revolver, felt the strong need of a whiskey and weaved my way toward the bar before recalling that there were three Fyfe brothers. I stopped, searched the saloon and saw the new faro dealer palming his revolver.

Things moved slowly, as if in a dream. I knew I'd never be able to match that man's draw. I watched in horror, saw everything clearly as his slender hands drew the pocket revolver from out of nowhere, the thumb jerk back the hammer, trigger finger squeeze, the burst of flame, heard the muffled roar. What I didn't feel, though, was a bullet rip through my chest.

Something crashed behind me. I whirled around. A dark-haired man who had been sitting at a corner table staggered, clutching his stomach with both hands. A Remington revolver lay on the floor. The man groaned, looked up, tried to move to the door, and I realized this was the last of the Fyfe brothers. Another gunshot exploded, and the wounded man jerked, gasped and pitched headfirst onto the floor, overturning a spittoon and staining Dottie Bagwell's floor with blood and tobacco juice.

When the smoke drifted away, the faro dealer smoothed his brocade vest, sat down and pushed up his black Stetson with the barrel of his revolver. "Jack Mackinnon, you need to learn to watch your back," Tenedore Keough said, smiling.

Since Jacksboro's marshal was in Weatherford, Dottie Bagwell ordered Ten and me to take the three dead men to Fort Richardson and report to a Captain Leviticus Miller at dawn. I didn't ask why, although I knew the Army had abandoned Fort Richardson earlier that year. You didn't argue with Dottie, so we did as we were told, throwing the Fyfe brothers in the back of a buckboard and riding to the Army post. Fulton's last shot had burned my throat a tad, and I had cut my thumb slightly on the Spiller and Burr's hammer, but those were my only injuries.

"I took your advice, Jack," Ten told me. "Got another line of work."

Those smoke-filled saloons won't help your lungs, I

thought, but didn't say anything. Then I realized I needed to tell Ten something. "Thanks," I said. He had saved my life.

He shrugged.

"Us Carolina boys have to stick together, my friend." He glanced at our lifeless cargo. "You're pretty handy with that revolver, Jack. I don't think you missed once."

I made Ten stop the wagon right then, dropped to the ground and left my supper and several whiskeys on a patch of prickly pear. Keough laughed when I climbed back into the seat. "You're as pale as me, amigo," he said, and urged the mules on to the fort.

At the edge of the post we found about twenty men, in civilian clothes, shoeing their mounts, eating breakfast and cleaning their weapons. A tall man with a gray beard and black broadcloth suit stepped out of a Sibley tent. The man looked like a telegraph pole, so skinny you could slide him into a rifle scabbard, about six-foot-six, all sinew and leathery skin with piercing gray eyes. Ten pulled up in front of him, tipped his hat and introduced ourselves.

"We were told to bring these gents in to a Captain Miller," Ten said. "We had a little disagreement at Dottie's last night, and the law's out of town. You know where we might find this Miller?"

The gray eyes never blinked. He glanced at the bloody bodies and studied us. I regretted not covering up the Fyfes. For a second, I thought I might throw up again.

"You've found him, boys. Now hand over your weapons."

Ten and I were thunderstruck. Half-expecting to be lynched, Keough pushed back his coattail, and covered the butt of his Colt, a move that got the attention of every man in camp. Five revolvers, two shotguns and thirteen Sharps rifles trained on us. Miller had never moved, but now he pulled back his own coat and revealed the small round badge pinned on the lapel of his vest. Stamped above and below a five-point star cut out in the center of the silver badge read: *Captain, Texas Rangers, Company G.*

The new Rangers were only four years old by then but had already earned a lethal reputation. You didn't go against the Rangers unless you were plumb loco or were going to hang anyway. I slowly drew the Spiller and Burr and handed it butt forward to the lanky captain. He took it, tossed it onto one of the Fyfe brothers and held out his palm. Those icy eyes locked on Ten. Keough reluctantly handed Miller his Colt. The captain nodded, pitched the gun into the buckboard and said, "We'll hold court inside."

"It was self-defense," I offered.

"I'll be the judge of that." He disappeared inside the canvas tent.

One of the Rangers smiled. "Judge, jury, executioner, and he'll read over your graves after he's hanged you. You boys are in for a treat."

Miller didn't swear us in. He just sat on a camp chair behind a folding wooden desk and filled his mouth with a wad of tobacco. Two guards holding Sharps followed us inside the tent and prodded us forward. Miller got his chaw into a comfortable position and said, "Remove your hats and state your names."

We did as we were told. Miller looked at me. "Speak."

I tried to swallow but couldn't. So I took a deep

breath, exhaled, and related my story. No lies, no exaggerations, just everything as I remembered. When I had finished, Miller nodded and turned his head. A spittoon in the corner rang loudly. The Ranger wiped his mouth and ordered Keough to tell his story. Ten started, but he wasn't halfway through when he took to coughing. When Miller saw the flecks of blood, his eyes registered the first emotion I had seen that morning.

"Get him out of my tent!" Miller yelled, and the two guards helped Ten outside. I started to go, but he stopped me with a sharp command. Miller spit again and called out for a Sergeant James. A blond-haired man stuck his head through the canvas door. "Bring me The Book," Miller ordered. A minute later, the sergeant returned with a small, paper-covered book titled *List of Fugitives From Justice.*

"What were the names of those men you killed?" Miller asked.

I told him, and Sergeant James whistled. "You killed all three of the Fyfe brothers."

"Just two of them. Ten Keough killed the other right before he was about to back-shoot me."

The sergeant told Miller, "See Trinity County, Captain."

Miller thumbed through the pages and read aloud: " 'Fyfe, Fulton: Theft of cattle (twelve indictments). Murder, convicted May '72, escaped. Instigating murder. Assault to murder. Threat to take life. Theft of horses. Is twenty-six years old, six feet high, weighs one-eighty pounds, crooked Roman nose, tolerably short upper lip, doesn't speak much unless spoken to, rough appearance, rougher character.' "

The sergeant nodded. "That's him, Captain. His brothers were just as bad. They're in The Book, too. Grayson County, I think."

"Those men in the buckboard. Are those the Fyfe brothers, Sergeant?"

"Yes sir. Couple of the boys recognized old Forbes. And Fulton's name was carved on the butts of his Colts. I'd say you can scratch the Fyfe brothers off the list, thanks to this here boy."

"Very good, Sergeant. See to the consumptive outside. And bring Mr. Mackinnon some coffee."

I relaxed as Captain Miller penciled a line through the name of Fulton Fyfe, found the other brothers's listings and scratched through their names as well. He looked up at me. I wasn't going to be hanged.

"Mr. Mackinnon," he said, "how would you like to join the Texas Rangers?"

Chapter Three

We stopped in Spanish Fort for two reasons. As the newest members of Miller's Ranger company, Ten and me needed to be outfitted. The great state of Texas paid us thirty-three dollars a month and found and furnished shells for our firearms, but we had to supply the weapons. Captain Miller was adamant on many things, primarily that we buy Sharps rifles and Colt revolvers. He had a friend in Spanish Fort who dealt in firearms, so we went there after he advanced us enough money for horses and saddles.

The town overlooked the Red River and supplied cowboys herding longhorns to Kansas, not to mention outlaws on the dodge heading into the Indian Territory. There were four hotels, a post office, two churches—Baptist and Methodist—no school and maybe twenty saloons. Five doctors hung their shingles in Spanish Fort, and all of them did steady business. So did the undertaker.

While most of the boys visited the Cowboy Saloon,

Sergeant Thaddeus James, Ten and me went into Iowa Glen's Gun Shop, a small frame building that smelled of oil and tobacco. A white-bearded man wearing spectacles sat behind a desk, staring at two old Colt revolvers, an 1860 Army and an 1851 Navy. He swore under his breath and considered us briefly.

James—Sergeant Thad, the boys called him—introduced us and told him our business. Iowa Glen nodded and said, "I only got one Sharps in. Hope Captain Miller don't get a burr under his saddle if I have to sell one of your new Rangers a Winchester instead."

"Captain Miller ain't fond of repeaters. Says they'll encourage a man to waste ammunition, and that costs the State money."

Glen shrugged. "Pick out what you want and see me when you're ready. I got a problem here to figure out."

I walked over to the desk and saw the cap-and-ball Colts. "You mind?" I asked and picked up the Navy. The cylinder rattled, it was so loose. Keeping my finger out of the trigger guard, I pulled the hammer back to full cock and rotated the cylinder, which you shouldn't be able to do. The Navy also needed a good cleaning. Specks of green stained the brass frame and backstrap. Shaking my head, I eased down the hammer, adjusted the cylinder and returned the revolver to the table.

"Brass frame tends to shoot itself loose after a while," I said. "That gun's in such poor condition, I don't know if it's even worth fixing."

Glen removed his glasses, glanced at the table and handed me the Army. "What about this one?"

Sergeant Thad laughed. "Mr. Glen, can't you fix guns?"

22 *Johnny D. Boggs*

"No," he snapped. "I sell the things. That's all I do. What about the Army, Ranger? Can you fix it?"

The hammer was at full cock and wouldn't budge. Nor would the trigger.

"You got a screwdriver?" I asked. Glen scrapped the legs of his chair against the floor and hurried behind a counter. "And a mainspring vise?" I called out.

He didn't have a vise, but I didn't need one. I disassembled the Colt, found the trigger mechanism and had the revolver ready to fire in less than ten minutes. Iowa Glen smiled. Sergeant Thad's head bobbed appreciatively. "How'd you learn that?" Thad asked.

I told him about my apprenticeship to a gunsmith in New Orleans. "Captain'll be pleased to have a gunsmith in the company," Sergeant Thad said. "And I reckon you can earn a few extra dollars helpin' the boys."

That I hadn't considered. The idea struck me as sound. After all, thirty-three dollars in State script wouldn't last long when I was about to be charged seventeen dollars for a Colt and who knew how much for a Sharps after already owing the State of Texas one-twenty-five for the blue roan gelding and Denver saddle purchased in Jacksboro. Iowa Glen gave me a slight discount, however, by trading in my Spiller and Burr and taking into consideration the work I did on the Army Colt.

I didn't get the Sharps, though. Ten picked it up first, so that left me with a Winchester carbine and a Frontier Colt revolver with a seven-and-a-half-inch barrel. Both weapons fired .44-40 ammunition, a convenience and cost-saving measure I hoped Captain Miller would appreciate. He didn't.

Like I said, we rode to Spanish Fort for two reasons,

the main one being the fact that rustlers had made off with some prime horses from S. W. Waggoner's ranch near St. Jo. Captain Miller figured the horse thieves would cross the Red River near Spanish Fort and hold up for a while until they could find a buyer. The Rangers had no jurisdiction in Indian Territory, but Captain Miller didn't care.

"When you hit a man with a Sharps, he stays down," Miller told me. "That Winchester is nothing but a toy. The first chance you get, you're trading it in for a Sharps. Understand me?"

"Yes sir."

Miller had a scout, spy, whatever you want to call him, named Javier Evaristo, a one-eyed Mexican with a fondness for smoking cigars and hanging outlaws. He braided the ropes himself, and bragged that they always snapped a man's neck so he didn't suffer—unless Javier didn't like the man; then he would make sure the killer choked to death.

We crossed the Red River that afternoon after Javier rode to Spanish Fort and informed Captain Miller of the outlaw camp's location. The horse thieves were careless. Their camp had been too easy to find, and most of the outlaws sat around a campfire, passing a clay jug around, laughing, singing, telling jokes. The horses were held in a rope corral, guarded by two sentries. I counted fifteen men.

"How you want to do this, Captain?" Sergeant Thad asked.

Miller tugged his beard for only a second. "Sergeant, take five men around back. I'll leave another five here.

The rest of us will charge in and kill them where they sit. Anyone who gets past us, shoot them dead. Our men will wear bandannas across our faces like bandits. Do not shoot anyone with a mask. Ranger Mackinnon?"

"Sir?"

"Since you are armed with a Winchester, you will ride with us into the camp. That repeater will be more useful killing at close range."

My first thought was to run, but instead I drew my new carbine from the scabbard, pulled my bandanna over my nose and glanced at Ten. He smiled. "Don't worry, Ranger Jack," he said. "I'll be right behind you."

What happened next has been told over and over again, first in Robin K. Hunter's *Ranger Glory; or The Thrilling Ride of Tenedore Keough and Jack Mackinnon*, and in other five-penny dreadfuls, dime novels and two fairly accurate—and forgotten—accounts in *Frank Leslie's Illustrated Weekly* and the *National Police Gazette*. All of the stories, however, stated that Ten Keough led the charge. Truthfully, I did, and it wasn't because of a sense of Ranger justice and Texas bravado.

My horse spooked.

Somebody fired. Maybe one of the thieves spotted us, maybe a Ranger just got careless, but at the loud crack, the roan loped straight for the outlaw camp. I lost my reins, almost lost my breakfast and let out a scream that some called a Rebel yell but was actually just a cry of terror. The outlaws scattered and started shooting. Bullets whined by thicker than mosquitoes. I remembered the Winchester I held, levered in a cartridge and fired, then cocked the carbine again. It occurred to me that the roan had no intention of stopping, so I freed my boots and went sailing. I landed feet first in the middle of the campfire, spreading smoke, hot coals and curses, and dived into the center of the camp. I looked up, saw a boot in front of my rifle barrel and jerked the trigger.

The outlaw dropped to the ground in agony. I rolled over, spit out sand and heard the whine of a bullet ricocheting near my head. Horses—stolen livestock, outlaws' saddle mounts and those of the charging Rangers—thundered through camp. Somehow, I managed to pull myself to my knees, jacked another shell into the Winchester and pulled the trigger again. I didn't bother to aim, just fired one way, then the other. Men and horses screamed. My ears began to ring. A bullet tugged on my hat. I jumped to my feet, saw a figure on horseback and aimed. I held my fire, recognizing the calico bandanna that covered Tenedore Keough's face. Right then, he looked like he belonged on the cover of a half-dime novel, sitting in the saddle, firing his Colt left and right, never blinking. When the .45 snapped on an empty chamber, he shoved the Colt into his holster and pulled the Sharps from the scabbard, aimed, shot, slid from the saddle and swung the heavy rifle like a club, breaking a charging rustler's stride and neck.

I whirled around, saw a man heading for me with a butcher knife and pulled the trigger. The Winchester was empty, and my assailant smiled. So I pitched him the carbine, and the fool instinctively caught the useless thing, dumbfounded. By the time he dropped the Winchester to continue his pursuit, I had drawn my Colt. He dropped to the earth, dead as he ever would be.

It was over in less than five minutes. I stood by the remains of the fire, surprised to be alive. Ten knelt, his chest heaving, fighting for breath, but he pulled down the bandanna and smiled, letting me know he would be fine. Right then, Captain Miller rode up, whipped off his hat and cut loose with a hurrah.

"By jingo, I knew you two men had the makings!" he yelled. "You charged in here like Comanches! Three cheers for Tenedore Keough and Jack Mackinnon!"

We had killed thirteen men and wounded two, the man I shot in the foot and a gut-shot Mexican who wouldn't live past sunset. One of the Rangers had a thumb shot off, another had a flesh wound in his left thigh, and I realized a bullet had cut a swath across my back. It bled a lot, but Sergeant Thad dabbed it with horse liniment, wrapped it with strips of my extra shirt and informed me that I would be ready to ride in no time. The liniment hurt worse than the bullet.

After the horses had been rounded up, and the dead bodies piled under a cottonwood, Captain Miller stared at the wounded man.

"I'll have your name," Captain Miller said.

The outlaw groaned and told the captain where he could go.

"You'll be there directly, mister. Now your name!"

The man relented. "Joe Bean of Wise County. If you're going to hang me, you son of Satan, I'd appreciate it if you'd write my ma, tell her where I'm planted."

Miller ignored him, flipped through The Book and frowned. "There's no Joe Bean listed in *Fugitives*. Are you lying to me?"

"No. I ain't no fugitive. Ain't wanted for nothing."

"Stealing horses is a crime. So is attempt to murder a Texas Ranger. Evaristo!"

Old Javier walked up, his good eye gleaming, enjoying a cigar. He held a hangman's noose in his right hand. *"El capitán, es muy bueno."*

"Get on with it. How's the other prisoner?"

Javier shrugged. "He will shout at the devil soon."

"Hang him anyway," Miller said. "I refuse to wait around for some horse thief to die."

I started to complain, but Sergeant Thad sternly informed me to keep my mouth shut.

"But Captain Miller can't just hang those men," I argued.

"Yes he can, Jack. And he will. It's called summary justice, and you remember one thing. Those men wouldn't give you no quarter if it was the other way around."

Captain Miller's report to Austin was accurate in most details, except for the location of the fight, which he claimed took place on the Texas side of the river. We took the recovered livestock to Waggoner's ranch, then retired to a saloon in St. Jo. Ten and I found a corner table and had consumed half a bottle of rye when a woman sat down beside us. She was no hurdy-gurdy girl, that was for sure. She wore a gray dress with some frilly stuff on the front and had her dark brown hair pinned up in the back topped with a flat-brimmed, flat-crown straw hat. I had never seen eyes so blue.

"Gentlemen, Captain Miller said I could have an interview with the two of you," she said, setting a pad and pencil on the table.

Ten and me looked at each other, then stared at the woman.

"You a newspaper reporter or something?" I asked.

She smiled. "Or something. I am Robin K. Hunter."

Chapter Four

This took place long before Robin Hunter made a name for himself/herself. You see, most folks thought Robin was a fellow until she took her talents to the stages in New York and Chicago, where she penned and produced a couple of horrible plays about the heroic frontiersmen Ten Keough and Ranger Jack. She hired a couple of thespians for the parts and never said why she didn't let Ten and me play ourselves.

I'm getting ahead of myself. In 1878, she had one half-dime novel to her credit, and she showed us a copy of *Dunn's Guns and the Lost Chief*. I read a couple of pages while Ten bought her a glass of wine.

"My editors liked my story," she informed us, "but thought I could do even better by seeking out real heroes on the frontier to write about them. Our readers back East can't get enough stories of the lawless West." She nodded at the novel I was reading. "Everything in that novel is straight from my head."

I passed the book to Ten. "You mean in that first chapter where Dave Dunn kills six men with his Patterson Colt, you just made all that up?"

"Yes." She beamed. "I did."

"No offense, ma'am, but a Patterson Colt only holds five rounds, and any gunman walking around these days with one of them relics ain't too smart."

Ten grunted. "Maybe he killed the sixth man by clubbing him to death."

"Nope. Read it. He shot him. Fact is, he shot some of those men more than once. Never even reloaded."

Robin sipped her wine. She never lost her smile. "That's right. Captain Miller said you were a gunsmith. Well, Ranger Jack, it's just fiction. Our readers don't care for accuracy. They just want a good story with plenty of action." She reached out and touched my right hand. "But with you helping me out, Jack, I bet I could get a great story."

I wished she hadn't let go of my hand, but she took her wineglass again. Well, I must have been smitten right then. Ten topped off my rye, and I sent it down neat. "Jack and me," he told Robin, "we got plenty of stories we could tell you."

She picked up her pencil. I never could blame Robin much for her novels' lack of veracity. Ten and me didn't help her set the record straight, especially on that first book. We was just drunk enough to give her a show. Somehow, she turned our slurred words and pack of lies into something folks from New York to Sacramento liked a whole lot.

"Were those horse thieves the first men you killed?" she asked.

"No, ma'am," Ten said. "We killed the Fyfe brothers back in Jacksboro. It was a fair fight."

She scribbled something down, nodding. "Yes, I recall reading something about that in the *Fort Worth Daily Standard.* They were notorious outlaws, right?"

"Murderers for sure," Ten said. "Vile and wicked, prone to ungentlemanly ways."

"Great," Robin said. "This is great, Ten."

I couldn't let my friend get all the glory. "There was ten of them," I lied.

But Ten was quicker. "And I killed seven."

I countered: "But two of mine was seven feet tall."

It went on like that, as you know if you've ever read *Ranger Glory.* The saloons didn't close in St. Jo, so we talked, drank and stretched the truth until dawn. Robin filled up two pads and had started on a third, when Ten stared into the sunlight. "Robin, would you like breakfast?"

"Certainly," she said.

I looked at the four empty whiskey and three wine bottles on the table. Ten struggled to his feet as Robin gathered her stuff. I sat like a stump, tried to move my legs, but they didn't want to work, and the thought of food made my stomach dance an Irish jig. Ten had trouble standing straight or still, but Robin looked as though she had been drinking lemonade all night.

"You coming, Jack?"

"No," I said. "Think I'll stay here a while."

When they had disappeared through the batwing doors, I called out to the bartender for some coffee. I thought I was having some drunken dream when Captain

Miller sat at the table and slid a tin cup of strong brew toward me.

" 'Morning, Ranger Jack," he said. "How was your interview?"

I tried to sip the coffee, but gagged instead, slumped onto the table and buried my face in my hands. The captain snorted. "So you and Ten are going to be heroes," he said mockingly. "Wild Bill Hickok and Ranger Jack Mackinnon mentioned in the same breath. You're pathetic, Mackinnon, not worth the badge I gave you. I figured that petticoat reporter might write about me. You know what she said, Jack? She said I was too old. Too old! I'm forty-nine, boy, rode with Captain Hays against the Comanches, fought against the Mexicans at Chapultepec and the Yankees with John Bell Hood's First Texas. And I'm too old. I've killed more men than you've ever known, Mackinnon, and I'll kill a passel more before I die."

He laughed bitterly, rose and left. This was the same man who had praised Ten and me for our actions against the horse thieves. I was too drunk to comprehend much of what he said at the time, but I knew things would never be the same between Captain Miller and me.

Captain Miller decided to make our company's headquarters near Spanish Fort. It was a good spot for the Rangers, close to the Indian Nations where owlhoots liked to hide and a good jumping-off spot to the rugged *Llano Estacado,* the Staked Plains that had once been a haven for Comanches. For a few months, we simply passed the time, went on a few patrols, and had to break up a wild fight between a couple of trail crews at the

Cowboy Saloon in town. Mostly, I worked on some guns, and Ten relieved a lot of Rangers of their money in faro games.

Right before Thanksgiving, after payday, Captain Miller had us ride to Spanish Fort to cut the dust and buy supplies. Mighty tired of eating our own cooking, Ten and me visited the Red River Hotel restaurant for a good steak and beans. The town was crowded, and folks packed the hotel like longhorn cattle in a Dodge City shipping yard. At the entrance to the restaurant, some gent holding a towel looked us over and frowned.

"You'll have to wait," he said.

"How long?" Ten asked.

The man shrugged. I guess he figured the Red River Hotel was too high and mighty for hardcases, and even when I pushed back my Mackinaw to reveal the Ranger badge, he wasn't impressed.

"How long?" Ten asked again.

"Thirty minutes. Maybe forty. Should I put you on the list?"

Ten looked at me. Shrugging, I suggested we could wait at the hotel bar. He liked that idea. "Sure," he told the gent. "The name's Ten Keough and Jack Mackinnon."

That fellow dropped the towel and begged our pardon, asked us if we could kindly wait for one minute, that he thought he might have something available immediately. He did, too, and Ten and me sat at table by the window overlooking Main Street. After serving us each a complimentary gin and bitters, the owner of the establishment asked to join us. A broad-chested man with red Dundreary whiskers, he said it was an honor to have us in his restaurant and promised to bring us cigars after our meals. We didn't know what was going on, but we kept quiet. Then the owner meekly asked if he might intrude, reached into his coat and pulled out a flimsy paper-bound novel. There it was—*Ranger Glory; or The Thrilling Ride of Tenedore Keough and Jack Mackinnon* by Robin K. Hunter, the first copy we had ever seen.

"Would you do me the honor of signing my copy?"

Grinning like schoolboys, we made our John Hancocks, wolfed down our meals, grabbed our free cigars, ran across the street to the mercantile and bought the last two copies of the half-dime novel that featured our likenesses on the cover. I had never read, or enjoyed, so much balderdash in all my years.

Ten and me hadn't seen Robin since August and had no idea a writer could churn out one hundred and eighty-seven pages so quickly, but it was right in front of our eyes. About a week later, a reporter from Dallas rode into camp and requested an interview with "the great Ten Keough and his trusty companion, Ranger Jack."

Trusty companion. That never quite set right with me, but I let it slide. Captain Miller was none too pleased about this latest intrusion, but he sent the reporter our way, and we talked to him for a good half-hour. When the next ink slinger dropped by camp, the captain cussed him out and told him to light a shuck back to Jacksboro. The reporter argued, so Captain Miller planted his foot on the man's backside to help him on his way.

"You boys best cut a wide path around Captain Miller," Sergeant Thad whispered, but Ten and me didn't really need the advice. And I was glad we didn't get to talk to the Jacksboro man. Fact was, I would be mighty

happy to get out on another scout, away from the hub-
bub. I changed my mind, though, in mid-December when
I found out Robin K. Hunter was in Spanish Fort. I had
hauled a German to the town jail for stealing a hog, and
she called my name when I stepped onto the boardwalk.
She sprinted from the hotel and leaped into my arms,
and we spun around as she giggled and planted her lips
on my cheek. Iowa Glen said I turned a mighty fine
shade of crimson.

"I'm so excited to see you. Is Ten around?" she practically squealed. I told her that Keough was back in
camp, and she grabbed my right arm and pulled me down
the boardwalk to Begoña's Café. She tossed three copies
of *Ranger Glory* and asked if I had seen a copy. I told
her Ten and me had bought two, and autographed about
twenty more in town.

"It's sensational," she said.

You got that right, I thought, but kept my mouth shut.

"My publisher wants to turn out more adventures
about you two," she said. "Some stores sold out in a day,
and I've had two newspaper reporters ask where they
can find you two."

"They found us," I said. "A guy from Jacksboro and
Dallas. Captain wouldn't let us talk to the—"

"Jack. Not Texas newspapers. They were from the
New York Tribune and the *Boston Daily Globe*. You're
famous. Nationally!" She paused long enough to sip her
tea. "How's Ten doing?" Her voice turned soft now.

"He's all right."

"The . . . the . . . lungs?"

There's no cure for consumption. She knew that.
Robin glanced at her drink. That must have been some

breakfast they had back in August. I wasn't the smartest man ever born, nor was I the most experienced man in the ways of women, but I knew right then that Robin K. Hunter was deeply in love with Dr. Tenedore Keough.

Ranger Jack, trusty companion. My heart broke. I felt like cussing till Christmas. I pulled off my hat and dropped it on the seat beside me. "Ten's doing better," I lied. "Staying out in camp, in the open air, seems to help his lungs." That was probably true, but Ten didn't spend much time out of doors. He'd visit Spanish Fort's gambling dens whenever he could find the time, pouring down rye like water, smoking cigars and hardly ever sleeping.

"So," she said, "you have any more exciting stories to tell me?"

"I just captured a big German who couldn't speak a word of English," I replied. "Theft of a hog."

Robin giggled, reached out and took both of my hands, squeezing them gently. My heartbreak ended. I laughed myself, and told her that her second book might not be as exciting as the first one.

"I've already finished the second book, Jack," she said. "It comes out next month. Come on, let's go find Ten."

Chapter Five

By the time Robin's second novel about Ten and me, *Ranger Revenge; or the Fyfe Brothers Strike Back*, hit the country, other publishing houses started printing their own adventures of Ten Keough and Ranger Jack. The first one was a pack of lies from Beadle's Half-Dime Library called *Heroes of the Border; or Trail to Doom*, in which Ten and Ranger Jack avenge Custer's death. That writer failed to comprehend that Ten and me had never been north of the Indian Nations and considered George A. Custer a dumb Yankee who got what he deserved. The Pocket Library put out a novel, too, and Keough and Mackinnon were featured in the *New York Weekly, Saturday Journal* and *Harper's Weekly* before long.

"Ten?" I asked one evening as we sat around the campfire at our Ranger headquarters. Ten was rolling a cigarette, which sure wouldn't help his lungs, and I was reading *Ranger Revenge*.

"Yeah."

"I thought we killed all the Fyfe brothers in *Ranger Glory*."

"We did."

"You must have only wounded a couple, 'cause some of them is madder than hornets in this tale."

Ten snorted, struck a match on his thumbnail and fired up his smoke. "Just like a Fyfe," he said, "to play possum like that."

We laughed, and I tossed Robin's novel into his lap. "How much money you reckon them books make?"

"For who? Robin?"

"No, Mark Twain. Of course, Robin."

He took a long drag, coughed slightly and swore. Ten inhaled deeply, flicked the unfinished cigarette into the fire and smiled. "You getting greedy, pard? Want to ask Robin to split the profits?"

"No. Just curious."

"Jack," he said, stretching his arms. "She gets the money. We get the glory."

A shadow fell across us, and I looked into Captain Miller's glaring gray eyes. "Why don't you Rangers cut the gab, saddle up and patrol the river? Check the brands of any herds crossing, make sure they ain't stolen. And ride all the way to Colbert's Ferry and back. That should keep you two heroes busy."

That's pretty much how things went for a while. The captain tried to keep us on the scout, far from Robin K. Hunter and her quick-writing pencils. 'Course, Ten managed to sneak into Spanish Fort every now and then to see her, leaving me to cover for him. And just like that, he stopped. It was like he completely quit caring for

Robin. One night, when he got a note from Sergeant Thad that Robin wanted to see him, Ten just smiled and tossed the paper into the fire. His coughing had gotten worse, more frequent, to where I thought it might be best if he left the river country and found a drier climate, take Robin with him.

He laughed when I suggested that, which got me mad.

"What's the matter with you? Here you got a beautiful woman who's in love with you and making you famous, and all you want to do is sit in smoke-filled shanties and drink and gamble all night. You act like you want to die."

His smile faded, and his voice turned harsh. "What of it, Jack? Tell me something, amigo. Why did you charge in there against those horse thieves?"

I tossed the dregs from my coffee cup onto the ground, pouted a mite and answered softly, "My horse spooked."

He didn't laugh, which I had expected. Instead, he asked, "You ever wonder why I followed you into that cauldron? Or why I sided with you against the Fyfe brothers? Or even why I pulled a gun on you in that dentist's office back in Dallas?"

My head shook slightly.

"You think I want to die coughing my lungs out, Jack?" His voice was quiet but animated, and his eyes flashed with anger. "A bullet's quicker."

Muttering a curse, I rose, looked down on him with contempt and said, "If you don't want to live, Ten, why don't you just stick that .45 in your mouth and pull the trigger?"

He laughed, pulled the makings from his vest pocket and began to roll a cigarette. "Now I understand," he said brightly. "This ain't about us, Jack. It's about her. You're jealous." He waved his arm toward Spanish Fort. "Go to her, pard. You have my blessing."

I cussed again and left him laughing, saddled my roan and took off to town. Robin was staying on the second floor of the Lone Star Hotel, and I found her in the room. She smiled when she opened the door, trying to pretend she hadn't been crying, but I knew from those eyes.

"Ten got stuck with guard duty," I lied. "Asked if I could . . ."

Well, that's why I wasn't good at lying, unless I was drunker than Gibson's goat and telling a pretty woman fanciful stories about shootouts with outlaw gangs and the like. "You had supper?"

We ate at the café, but neither of us done much damage to our plates. Mostly we just sat around, talking about nothing, though she tried briefly to coax a story for her next Wide Awake novel out of me. I didn't help much.

At last, she looked up at me with those stunning blue eyes, reached across the table and took my hands in hers. "Do you ever get mad at him, Jack?"

"He can make a body sore."

I pulled away just so I could cover her hands, squeezed them and said, "He's no good for you, Robin. I mean, Ten's my best friend, but he ain't never gonna make you happy."

"I know."

We walked silently back to the hotel, and I opened the door for her. She stood in the doorway, forced a smile and thanked me for supper. A cattleman stumbled up the stairs, begged our pardon and struggled with his key before practically falling into his room and slamming the door shut. Robin and I didn't move until we heard him snoring a few minutes later. Our eyes met, and I leaned forward, but she placed two fingers on my lips, whispering, "Don't."

She was about to cry. I held her while she trembled, feeling like a double-dealing card shark. That didn't stop me. Robin fell into my arms, and when she looked up, we kissed.

"Oh, Ten," she said softly and pulled away in horror. "I'm so sorry, Jack. I didn't mean . . ."

I kissed her again to let her know it was all right. She fell against my chest and hugged me tightly. "Jack," she whispered. "Whatever you do, don't fall in love with me."

I couldn't tell her it was too late.

Robin and me saw each other a few more times over the next few weeks. And Ten? He didn't care. He even seen us once, when he was stepping out of the Cowboy Saloon. All he did was smile and tip his hat as we walked to the Red River Hotel restaurant. Captain Miller watched us, too, only he didn't tip his hat or smile.

"You're good for Robin, Jack," Ten told me on a scout one time. "She deserves somebody decent . . ." He cussed himself and spit out a bloody froth. "Somebody with good lungs."

I didn't say nothing. Ten did love Robin. I was sure of that, and Robin loved Ten, not me. And good old John "Jack" Lindsay Mackinnon? He was stuck in the middle of this romantic triangle, Shakespearean tragedy, whatever you wanted to call it. On Palm Sunday, in my store-bought broadcloth suit and black tie, I escorted Robin Hunter to the Baptist church where I learned that in addition to being a talented writer, she also had an amazing voice. I was plumb sorry she got stuck with a Texas Ranger who couldn't carry a tune in a war bag.

I autographed copies of Robin's *Texas Cyclone; or, Rangers on the Prod* for a couple of schoolboys after the services and walked Robin down the boardwalk for dinner at the Red River Hotel. Only three dusty men standing in the middle of Main Street called us to a halt.

"So you're the famous Ranger Jack," one of the men said as the wind pushed the wide brim of his hat against the crown. He had dark hair and a well-waxed mustache, and pushed back his linen duster so he could rest his right hand on the butt of his Remington revolver.

The second man, a bucktoothed, bearded piece of trash in brogans, laughed. "And this must be his lady fair."

"Lady fair?" the first man said. "You mean painted lady."

I started to step off the boardwalk, but Robin grabbed my arm. "Don't," she pleaded. "It doesn't bother me."

The first man howled. "Oh, listen to mama, Ranger Jack. Run along and hide."

"It bothers me," I told Robin, and stepped onto the street.

Bucktooth smiled and put his thumbs in his waistband close to the Spiller and Burr stuck in his right pocket. I wondered if that was my old revolver. The first man licked his lips, spread his legs and said, "Well, Ranger Jack, I reckon you're a man after all." The third man, a Mexican vaquero, turned pale and didn't say a word.

"You will apologize to the lady," I said.

Bucktooth and Big Mustache laughed until I unbuttoned my frock coat and pushed it back, revealing the .44-40 Colt holstered across my belly. Usually, I wore my holster on my right hip but didn't want the Colt bumping on the church pew so I slid it over, else they would have been able to realize I was Ranger-dressed. I reckon they didn't think a man would wear a gun to church, but Captain Miller issued us standing orders that we go heeled at all times, all places.

"Let's go," the Mexican said. "Come on. It's not worth it. *Por favor.*"

Big Mustache lost his sass and color, Bucktooth turned away, and for a second I thought it was over. Suddenly, Bucktooth let an oath fly and spun around, jerking the Spiller and Burr with his right hand. I would have been dead if Bucktooth's gunsight hadn't snagged on his trousers. Turning sideways, I drew, thumbed back the hammer and put a slug in Bucktooth's chest. He shot himself in the foot and collapsed into the dust without even a sigh.

Big Mustache crouched and jerked his Colt. Keeping my feet planted, I swung my revolver around and ordered him to stop. He didn't listen, so I pulled the trigger. He staggered back, but managed to level his revolver. Our guns roared at the same time. He missed. I didn't.

I watched as he dropped to his knees, straightened with a groan and brought the gun up once more. The .44-40 boomed again, and Big Mustache yelled and fell to his side in a pool of blood. I saw the kids then, standing on the boardwalk, one covering his ears, the other's mouth wide open, horror etched on their faces. I couldn't hear anything but the ringing in my ears, but I knew both boys were crying—the same kids I had signed copies of *Texas Cyclone* for just minutes earlier.

The boardwalks seemed full of people, all in their Sunday best, most of them looking at me. Some seemed to be crying. One man covered his children with his own body. An elderly woman cautiously peered over a rain barrel. A girl pulled herself out of the water trough, her white dress ruined. Others ran down the street, away from the shooting. I found Robin and saw her eyes roll back as she fell backward into Iowa Glen's arms. He studied her briefly, faced me and mouthed the words, "She's just fainted, Jack."

I couldn't hear a thing until the ringing stopped and a baby's wail pierced my ears.

Blazing pain tore through my left side as the roar echoed in my ears. I dropped to my knees with a curse.

The Mexican. I had forgotten all about him, never considered him a threat, but I twisted to see him sprinting across the street, firing again. My left hand gripped my side, sticky and warm with blood. I cocked the Colt and fired, knew I had missed, thumbed back the hammer, pulled the trigger and heard the loud snap that told me my revolver was empty. The Mexican disappeared into the livery.

I struggled to my feet, shucking out the empty casings and reloading as I stumbled across the street. My mouth felt dry, and sweat poured down my forehead. It hurt to breathe. As the sixth bullet slid into the last chamber, I snapped the cylinder gate shut and fell against the side of the livery stable, just beside the open doorway. I pulled the hammer to full cock and tried to steady my nerves, stop shaking.

I lifted my coat away with my bloody left hand and glanced at the wound. I didn't like its looks, didn't like how much I had bled, knew I couldn't stay conscious much longer. Next I knocked off my hat and wiped the sweat from my forehead, trying to summon the nerve and energy to move into the livery. I listened, heard voices and became confused.

"Por favor," a voice cried out. *"¡Dios, no!"* Then, the same voice, in English: "Please, Captain Ranger, I am sorry. I surrender."

I moved into the stable and saw the vaquero on his knees, hands above his head, crying. Before him stood Captain Miller, his long arm holding his Colt just inches from the Mexican's forehead.

"No fue culpa mía," the vaquero begged.

Captain Miller barely even considered me, stared at the Mexican and pulled the trigger. As he walked outside and holstered his revolver, I shuddered at his dry voice: "See if Miss Hunter will put that in her next book."

Chapter Six

My eyes opened. The face slowly came into focus. I had a bad case of cottonmouth, and my left side felt like somebody had slapped a branding iron to it. I coughed twice and tried to sit up but quickly gave up. Eventually, I realized the smiling face in front of me belonged to Texas Ranger Tenedore Keough. A cigarette dangled from his lips as he shuffled a deck of paste cards and dealt a round of solitaire stud poker, using my chest for a table.

"How you feel, amigo?" he asked.

When I told him, he laughed.

"Well, you were in mighty good hands. Every doctor in town wanted the opportunity to save your life. Sergeant Thad and me practically had to fight the unlucky ones off with sticks. I thought about cutting you myself, but, alas, Charles Dennis Tenedore Keough is licensed only as a dentist."

I attempted a joke. "You couldn't even pull my tooth, remember?"

Ten dealt another card, smirked and said, "Ace high. I win again." After collecting and shuffling the cards, he played another hand before telling me: "The bullet's out, though. You should be ready to ride in no time."

The doctor came in, changed the bandages—which interrupted Ten's card game—and said I was "a crackerjack healer." Doc Harker was a tall man with a bad haircut and the biggest ears I ever saw. He looked disheveled, uneasy—*This is the doctor Ten picked for me*, I thought, then quit complaining. I was alive. The doc tried to explain the bullet's path through my side, the damage it had done, how lucky I was to be alive. Before leaving, Harker poured me a glass of water, which Ten offered to freshen up with his flask. I declined.

Slowly, the memories of the shootout came back. Ten told me I had been out for almost four days, that the telegraph office had been flooded with wires asking about my well-being. One came from the governor, and another from Buffalo Bill Cody, who said he was a big fan of Robin K. Hunter's novels.

"You trying to hog all of the glory, pard?" Ten asked while dealing another hand of poker. "Not smart, Jack. Remember, if I would have been there, that Mexican wouldn't have shot you. Watch your back. Remember?"

I started to laugh, but the vision of the pleading vaquero flashed before my eyes.

"He killed him, Ten," I said. "Captain Miller shot down that Mexican like a dog."

Frowning, Ten gathered the cards and stuck the deck inside his gray frock coat. "I know," he said. "Ol' Anse Deweese at the livery saw the whole thing. He had been sleeping off a drunk in the loft. Anse told me and Sergeant Thad, and we told him to keep his mouth shut, forget the whole thing."

"Why?"

Ten grinned. "Because Anse is terrible at faro, and I don't want the captain to kill him, too. It would ruin my profits."

I didn't find that amusing. I sipped my water and asked about Robin. Ten looked away and drank from his flask. I remembered her fainting, but suddenly felt chilled, struck with fear. A stray bullet? Almost crying, I begged Ten to tell me. He capped the flask, slid it into his coat pocket and handed me an envelope. I recognized Robin's flowery handwriting.

"She's all right, Jack," he said. "Asked me to give you this."

After fighting to get the letter from the envelope, I read:

My dearest Jack:

Forgive me for lacking the courage to tell you good-bye. Doctor Harker assures me that you will recover, and I would not go unless I knew this. After what happened, though, I need time away from here, time to get my thoughts in order. To write about violence is one thing; to see it in person, on the streets, to see you gravely wounded, that is a nightmare which shall never leave my mind. My sister lives in St. Louis and has invited me to stay with her. I am leaving today by stagecoach.

Oh, darling, one day you'll find a girl, some corn-fed farmer's daughter perhaps, or better yet, the favorite daughter of a wealthy cattle baron.

She'll make you happy. But I am not that woman.
I cannot make anyone happy, and I'm afraid that,
after what happened here, I might end up getting
you and Ten killed. Thanks for your kindness, your
friendship, your love. Please watch over Ten. He
needs you. Above all, please take care of yourself.
Love,
Robin

I folded the letter and sank deep into my pillow. "She
rode out yesterday," Ten said. "On the stage to Colbert's
Ferry. Wouldn't tell me where she was bound."

"St. Louis," I said. "She has a sister there."

Ten scratched his nose. "Well, she'll probably make
you the hero and me the trusty companion in her next
novel. *Ranger Jack, Hero of Spanish Fort.* What would
you think of that, amigo?"

"She won't write anything about what happened," I
said softly.

She didn't. Fact is, no one wrote about the gunfight
at Spanish Fort except for a paragraph in an Austin paper
and an even shorter account in *Harper's Weekly* that said
*"Texas Ranger Jack Mackinnon was wounded in a gun
battle with outlaws in Texas. His assailants were sub-
dued, and Mr. Mackinnon will recover."* Certainly there
were printed stories about Ten Keough's and Ranger
Jack's shootouts with bandits, but Spanish Fort was
never mentioned, and none of the reconstructed gunplay
resembled what I had seen on Main Street that Sunday.
In time, the incident faded away. Spanish Fort had no
newspaper, and Captain Miller never bothered to send in

a report. When Austin demanded Captain Miller file one, he simply used the telegram as tobacco paper.

A week after Robin left Spanish Fort, I could get out of bed and move around, and even played a few rounds of poker with Ten in the hotel room. Sergeant Thad and some of the boys came up to visit and chastise me for getting out of Ranger duty, and the town mayor and leading citizens presented me with a new pair of boots made by Mr. H. J. Justin and a matched set of nickel-plated, ivory-handled, scroll-engraved Colt Peacemakers that must have set them back a hundred dollars.

"Anytime you decide to leave the Rangers, Mr. Mackinnon," the mayor said, "you just let us know, because we need a good marshal in Spanish Fort."

The last marshal had been shot dead a month before in a misunderstanding at the Cowboy Saloon. Being a town lawman didn't seem much better than being a Ranger.

Next a pretty little girl, in her best dress and with curled blond hair in ribbons, handed me a bouquet of bluebonnets, kissed my cheek and said in a timid, rehearsed speech: "Please get well, Ranger Jack. We won't forget what you have done for us."

They already have, I thought. Maybe they could ignore what had happened on Palm Sunday. Maybe they could conveniently block out visions of their children crying, screaming, witnessing men gunned down in the middle of the street right after church. I couldn't. I wouldn't. Ranger Jack, hero? I hadn't stepped onto Main Street to kill anybody, had hoped they would back down, but I knew the consequences. Now, three men were dead.

And over what? An insult or two. It definitely wasn't justice. And all I had accomplished was running off Robin Hunter.

Still, I pretended to be happy with the fanfare and said I couldn't wait to try on Mr. Justin's boots but those Colts looked too pretty to shoot. After shaking a dozen hands, I watched the parade file out of my room. Then I turned to Ten and asked if he would bring me a bottle.

"You feel like riding?"

I was sitting up in my bed, eating breakfast with Ten, when Captain Miller ducked into the room. Those hard eyes locked on me, and I saw him standing over that vaquero again, pulling the trigger and walking past me with that callous comment. *"See if Miss Hunter will put that in her next book."*

I hadn't seen him since.

"That bullet hole hasn't completely—" Ten began, but the captain waved his hand.

"Bosh," he said. "One .45 slug can't stop my hard-charging Ranger Jack. Your horse is waiting out front, Mackinnon. Yours, too, Keough. The Fort Worth stage was robbed last night, the messenger killed. Evaristo and Sergeant James are looking for tracks. Let's go."

Ten started to protest, but I swung out of bed. The quick movement almost made me pass out, but the dizziness faded and I said, "We'll be there as soon as I'm dressed, Captain," and reached for my trousers.

"Good." Captain Miller closed the door behind him.

Just pulling on my boots left me weak, and the gunbelt rubbed against my wounded side so much that I had to unbuckle the belt and shove the .44-40 into my left boot top. Ten gestured to the matching set of Colts.

"What about them?" he asked.

When I shook my head, he picked up the embossed holsters and belt. "You mind if I wear them?"

"Suit yourself."

I found a clean shirt, vest and bandanna and jammed my hat on my head. Turning around, I shook my head. Ten opened his coat to reveal the revolvers. Once again, he looked like he belonged on the cover of a Wide Awake novel.

"How do I look?" he asked.

"Like the procurer of a New Orleans bagnio," I answered, though I had never seen neither one.

Ten laughed and shook his head. "Well, I look better than you, Jack. You won't last half a day in the saddle. Stay—"

"You know the captain," I said. "You don't tell him no."

We walked outside and mounted our horses, not knowing it would be the last time Ten and me would ride together for a long time.

Chapter Seven

Javier Evaristo's one eye gleamed as he stuck a cigar in his mouth and leaned forward in the saddle. He didn't light the tobacco right then. I reckon he just wanted to savor the taste a spell. *"Muy pronto,"* he told no one in particular. "These men do not take time to cover their tracks. We find them soon."

Sergeant Thad muttered an oath. "Those tracks are headin' for the Nations. *Muy pronto* they'll be out of Texas."

Javier shrugged. "Who's to say what river that is? *¿Sí, el capitán?*"

"Shut up," Captain Miller snapped.

Javier was right, though. The tracks were easy to follow, heading north to the Red River on the main road. But they turned off the trail unexpectedly and moved west toward a small jacal and corral a few hundred yards away. We reined up, and the captain pulled a spyglass from his saddlebags to study the place. While he watched, Ten nudged his horse alongside mine and whispered, "How you holding up, amigo?"

My shirt stuck to my side from where the bullet wound had opened again. I felt weak and thought I might drop from my saddle at any second, or lose my breakfast on the withers of my roan. My heads were clammy and sweat burned my eyes, but I faked a smile and said, "I'll be fine."

Ten grunted something, glanced at Captain Miller and said, "If the shooting starts, you stay back. Ain't no point in getting yourself killed trying to prove something to the likes of him."

"Three men at the corral," the captain said, adding with contempt, "Mexicans."

"Stage driver and passengers said they seen six men in the holdup," Sergeant Thad said.

"Others could be hiding," a Ranger named O'Brien said. "Could be a trap."

Sergeant Thad, who had studied the jacal through the long brass telescope on his Sharps rifle, shook his head. "I don't think so. Looks like a bunch of farmers to me."

O'Brien agreed. "Yeah. Wouldn't make much sense for a bunch of outlaws runnin' from a hangman's rope to stop this close to the river."

Miller returned the brass scope to the saddlebag and urged his horse forward. "We'll find out soon enough, boys," he said. And we followed him.

A white-haired man with a flowing goatee and two boys, maybe in their late teens, left the corral and stood in front of the jacal as we rode up. The old-timer smiled, raised his right hand and greeted us in Spanish. We reined up, forming a semicircle around the Mexicans, and the friendliness vanished.

"Evaristo," Captain Miller said quietly.

Javier dismounted, withdrew his cigar and said, "We are Texas Rangers, pursuing six men who robbed a stagecoach and murdered a man on the Fort Worth road. Their trail leads to this ranch. *¿Comprende usted?*"

The man shook his head. *"Yo no comprendo."*

With a curse, Javier sent a rapid stream of Spanish. The eyes of the man and boys widened, and the old man answered.

Smiling, Javier said, "He says six men rode up this morning to water their horses."

"When they're this close to the river?"

Javier translated the question, and the man, now trembling, replied hurriedly, gesturing wildly. As the man spoke, Captain Miller ordered Ten and O'Brien to check the horses in the corral. I gripped the saddle horn to stay seated and waited for the Mexican to finish.

When the man fell silent, Javier said: "He says he thought the men were very drunk, says he believes they rode here to see if a woman might be handy, but, alas, there is only this peasant and his two sons."

"And he just let them go?" Miller swore underneath his breath.

Javier laughed. "The peasant says he could do nothing even if he had known those men were evil. After all, they are just one old man and two boys who have not seen their sixteenth birthdays. He begs us to forgive him for his cowardice, says we are welcome to water and feed our horses before continuing our pursuit of those wicked men."

The captain tugged on his beard, keeping his eyes trained on the three Mexicans, and called out: "What about that stock?"

"Pretty good horses, Captain," O'Brien replied. "Don't recognize the brand."

Javier asked about the horses. The man answered.

"He says they come from Mexico. A wedding present from the brother of his late wife."

The captain shook his head. "Well, I'll just call them stolen. Tell him that the Texas Rangers don't tolerate dirt-dwelling Mexicans who help killers escape justice. Get three ropes, Evaristo."

I saw the young Mexican in Anse Deweese's Livery Stable again, pleading for his life, saw Captain Miller's long-barreled Colt flash and the vaquero slam against a stack of bloodstained hay. I blinked.

The old man must have realized what was happening, because he dropped to his knees, hands clasped together, tears streaming down his eyes, begging for our mercy. Ten and O'Brien stood motionless by the corral. Sergeant Thad bowed his head, and a couple of the boys grinned. No one else moved until I slid off the roan and staggered in front of the family.

"You can't do this, Captain," I said.

Captain Miller laughed. "Are you going to stop me, Ranger Jack?" He swung around in the saddle and found Ten, then turned back to me. "Your partner doesn't appear willing to back your play. If you've no stomach for justice, hand me your badge, Mackinnon, and step aside."

"No. I won't let you do this."

Come on Thad, Ten, O'Brien. But they didn't move.

Miller roared again, slapped his thigh and said, "You're letting them five-penny dreadfuls go to your head, boy. Look at yourself. You're bleeding like a stuck pig, and you can't even reach that hogleg in your boot." The smile vanished. His gray eyes turned colder. "Make your play, Mackinnon."

I bent for the Colt, grimacing as pain shot through my side, and gripped the revolver's butt. I heard the hoof-beats, looked up as I eared back the hammer and saw the black boot swing from Captain Miller's stirrup.

The next thing I knew, I was crawling across the ground, my nose pouring blood, vision blurred. The old man's voice sang out a prayer, and one of his sons seemed to be crying. Spurs chimed, leather creaked and footsteps approached me. "Ten," I tried to call out, but managed only a sharp cry of pain.

"I'm gonna teach you a lesson, Ranger Jack."

A nightmare of agony shot through my chest. I fought for breath, gasped, tasted blood in my mouth. Strong hands ripped my shirtfront as I was jerked into a seated position that sent a river of blood and pain plunging from the bullet hole in my side. Hot breath that smelled of whiskey scalded my bloody nose. The gray beard and hard eyes became clear for a second, then something hard slammed against my head.

I lay on a cot, too scared to move. Texas or South Carolina, Heaven or Purgatory, I knew not which, nor did I care. In time, an hour, a day, a week—who knew?—I understood I was inside the jacal. A noise out-side commanded my attention. The door opened. Black eyes stared down at me. Cool water touched my lips, spilled down my throat. I coughed, groaned, begged for more water.

She knelt beside me, squeezing a wet bandanna over my mouth. Her cool hands wiped the water off my chin and cheeks. I recognized her, but it took a while to place the black hair. She worked at the Cowboy Saloon. I had seen her in Ten's arms a few times.

"How long?" I asked.

"Yo no comprendo."

I sighed, fell asleep. When I woke up, she smiled timidly and handed me a note.

Jack,

 Your horse is hobbled by the river. I'll try to send Iowa Glen or Doc Harker soon, but don't wait long. Miller might be back. Sorry that's all I can do for you. Good-bye.
Ten

Somehow I sat up and caught my breath. The girl stared at me in horror, or maybe disbelief. I held out my hand. She stepped back. *"Por favor,"* I said. "I can't stay here. Help me to the river." She didn't move. *"El río,"* I said again. *"Socorro. Por favor."* And that was about the limit of my Spanish. Her hands grabbed mine, pulled me to my feet, and we pitched and wheeled our way into sunlight.

I leaned against her as we moved north, knowing I couldn't fall. If I did, I wasn't sure I would get up again, even if the girl helped. We found a path through the brush and brambles. I slipped in the reddish-brown mud, and we tumbled to the river bank. The flowing water sounded heavenly. I wanted to drag myself to the edge and drink. The girl screamed. I rolled over and saw the three bodies hanging from the thickest limb of a cotton-wood.

A sign had been draped across the body of the old man.

HORSE THIEVES
HANGED BY TEXAS RANGERS
OUTLAWS BEWARE

The girl took off running down the riverbank. I reached for her, tried to beg her to stop and collapsed in the mud. I thought about Robin, then nothing at all.

The room smelled of tobacco and oil, and I recognized the scent before a stronger odor took hold. Chicken. Soup. Iowa Glen sat beside me, held a spoon under my nose. "You reckon you can try to get this down?"

I nodded and then didn't remember anything for an eternity.

"Who knows I'm here?" I asked.

"Doc Harker's been here a couple of times," Iowa Glen replied. "Mayor Boeke. We've tried to keep things quiet. Captain Miller's still in town, demanding free whiskey for his Rangers and pretty much slanderin' your name."

"How did I get here?"

"Ten Keough left me a message, but I had a hard time finding you. First I thought you was a goner, that Captain Miller had hanged your sorry carcass. Finally found your horse, hobbled where Ten said it would be, went down-stream and found you half-dead."

I polished off the chicken broth. "I thought you were Captain Miller's friend."

Glen laughed. "I tolerate the captain, much like every-body around here has to. But I like you, Jack. I'd prob-ably like you even if you hadn't fixed that old Army Colt."

"Where's Ten?" I asked.

"You forget about him."

I couldn't put off my question any longer. "Is he alive?"

Glen frowned but nodded. "Last I heard, he was still breathin'. Get some sleep. We'll talk directly."

I fell against the wooden wall but managed to keep my feet before Iowa Glen charged into the supply room and almost took my head off with the door. He helped me back to bed, cussing me out the whole time.

"Jack, you'll kill yourself."

I shuddered, waited for my breathing to calm and asked Iowa Glen if Spanish Fort had a new marshal yet.

He sighed. "You can't even walk, Jack."

"Answer me."

"No."

"Could you ask the mayor to come here?"

"Jack . . ."

"Please."

"All right, Jack. But you might not like your first job."

My first job, I thought, would be to arrest Captain Miller or at least run him out of Spanish Fort. I looked up at Iowa Glen, waiting. He took off his glasses, sighed and said, "Ten Keough's wanted for murder."

Chapter Eight

Five hundred dollars
REWARD!
THE STATE OF TEXAS
WILL PAY
FIVE HUNDRED DOLLARS
For the arrest and conviction of Tenedore Keough
for the murder of Anse Deweese of Spanish Fort,
Texas, on the thirteenth day of May in the year of
our Lord 1879. By order of
Leviticus A. Miller
Captain, Texas Rangers

I folded the placard and sighed. "Well, at least it ain't Dead or Alive."

Iowa Glen shook his head. "The understanding, unwritten of course, is that Captain Miller would prefer him brought in dead."

"Ten didn't kill Anse," I said softly.

61

"That mean ol' scout of the captain's, Evaristo, says he did. And Anse owed Ten a good chunk of money from the faro games. That scout says they took to arguin' in the livery, then Ten shot him down. Miller also says Ten shot Sergeant Thad in the back. Don't know why that ain't on the wanted poster."

"Is Thad dead?"

"Might as well be. His sister come up to fetch him home to Tyler. He ain't woke up since he got shot, though. They don't expect him to live."

Ten had left Texas in a hurry once word got out that he was wanted. I wondered where he would go. St. Louis? But I knew he had not committed murder. That wasn't Ten's style. Captain Miller had killed Anse Deweese, or had Javier do it for him, after somehow finding out the livery stable owner had seen him shoot that vaquero dead on Palm Sunday. One of them had also shot Sergeant Thad. I doubted if a Texas jury would ever convict Miller of murdering that vaquero, but figured the captain didn't want his reputation tarnished even the slightest. When I told Iowa Glen this, he just shook his head.

"You seen him shoot the Mexican. You could swear out a complaint."

"No," I said softly. "Folks would think I was just lying to help out Ten."

"Yeah, I reckon you're right. You ought to high-tail it out of Texas yourself, get as far away from Levi Miller as you can."

"Where would I go? St. Louis?" I thought of Robin again.

He shrugged. "Never been there. Hear it's a mighty fine city."

"No. I don't think I would like St. Louis. I'll stay here, for a while."

"Well, you still want me to fetch Mayor Boeke? You still interested in our marshal's job?"

I chuckled. "I'm out of work, need a job, and you won't pay me enough as a gunsmith." Iowa Glen laughed and walked to the door. I told him I also would appreciate the loan of a revolver. And a shotgun. Double barrel.

He nodded slightly. "Sure, Jack. But if you go against Levi Miller, all the guns I got ain't gonna do you a world of good."

The badge was plain, a tin star with five rounded points, stamped MARSHAL. The revolver was a Richards conversion of an 1851 Navy Colt, and the shotgun was a sawed-off Parker. I felt ready for Levi Miller, only he was long gone by the time I could walk up and down Main Street. The Rangers were off chasing outlaws in the Panhandle, and since most of the trail herds had crossed the Red River by now, or were moving farther west, Spanish Fort turned quiet.

In my first act as town marshal, I placed a sign on both roads entering town:

THE CARRYING OF FIREARMS

IN TOWN LIMITS

IS PROHIBITED.

FINE: $50

Mayor Boeke didn't like that at all. He argued that Spanish Fort had a lot of competition from other towns, that we needed the business especially since the trail herds were moving farther west, and cowboys liked towns where they could keep their weapons. Shooting out streetlights or puncturing the ceiling in the Cowboy Saloon seemed a small price for the business brought in.

"How many people are buried up on Boot Hill?" I asked.

He said he had no idea, so I informed him. "Forty-three. Three committed suicide. The other forty were killed." I should know. I had killed two of them myself.

"But . . ."

"Mayor, Dodge City doesn't allow firearms in the city proper. Most cowtowns don't. I agree the cowboys bring in business, but think about this. Everyone who wears a gun will pay fifty dollars to get out of jail. We'll confiscate the revolver. If he wants that back, he'll have to pay another ten dollars."

Boeke's eyes glinted. He suggested we make the "repossession fee" ten dollars for a revolver or derringer, fifteen for a shotgun and twenty for a rifle. I agreed. "Plus court costs," he said.

We shook hands on the deal.

The first novel painting Ten Keough as a ruthless outlaw came out in August, and it cost a whole dime. The memory of Ranger Jack quickly faded away, but Ten stayed in the news. He killed two men in Ogallala, Nebraska, in September. The wire said the men had been "part-time peace officers." I figured another term was more fitting: Bounty hunters.

For me, keeping order in Spanish Fort didn't prove difficult. I helped a few drunks to jail, disarmed a lot of visitors and collected the fines, and removed dead animals from the streets and alleys. For this, I received fifty cents for each animal I buried, be it rat or horse, and fifty dollars a month. Mayor Boeke and the Town Council kept all of the fines, not to mention the money I had to collect as licensing fees from gambling halls and saloons. I had a long way to go in business. A lot of lawmen got a percentage of fines and fees.

I was asleep at my desk one October afternoon when a squat Mexican barged in and fell to his knees, screaming, begging for me to do something. "English!" I said. "In English, *por favor*. And slowly."

He looked over his shoulder, stood and slammed the door shut. His chest heaved. He mumbled something in Spanish, and I was about to get an interpreter when he grabbed my arms and pleaded with me not to open the door. His words came out in broken English.

"*Señor* Marshal. Please. I beg of you. *El capitán* after me. He shot my horse. *Me hice daño en el tobillo.*" He pointed down. His left ankle was bleeding. "I run anyway. *Aquí.* Lock up me. *Yo soy Roberto Rueda.* I steal horses. Arrest me. *Por favor.* Don't let *el capitán* hang me."

Understanding, or guessing, what was happening, I shoved wanted horse thief Roberto Rueda in the cell, locked the door as he thanked me profusely and pulled the Parker from the gun rack. I opened the breech, shoved in two shells of buckshot and stepped outside just as Levi Miller and ten Rangers rode up.

Miller's shock didn't last long. He recovered and laughed.

"It's Ranger Jack, boys!" He pointed to the badge and corrected himself. "Make that Marshal Mackinnon. How are you, Jack? It's been a while."

"We have an ordinance against the carrying of firearms, Miller," I said. "Drop the guns or get out of Spanish Fort."

Miller shook his head. "That sounds like a line straight out of one of Robin K. Hunter's novels. She hasn't written anything in a while." He gripped the saddle horn and leaned forward. "We're on business, Marshal. In hot pursuit of a Mexican horse thief. Roberto Rueda is listed in The Book. Jack County. I aim to have him."

"He's not a fugitive if he's in jail," I said. "I have him."

Miller slapped his thigh. "That's just like you, Mackinnon. Always protecting the Mexicans. But I want that miserable horse thief, Jack. Now."

"Come and get him." I thumbed back the hammers on the Parker, brought the stock to my shoulder and looked down the barrel at Levi Miller's bearded face.

For a second, I thought about pulling the trigger.

Then Mayor Boeke stepped off the boardwalk. "Captain," he said nervously, glancing sideways at me. "It's good to see you and the boys. Let's go on to the Cowboy Saloon. The first drink's on Spanish Fort. What do you say, Rangers?"

"What about our weapons?" someone asked.

Boeke laughed, his humor strained. "Just a misunderstanding is all. The ordinance doesn't apply to lawmen such as yourselves. Come on."

O'Brien pulled up alongside Miller. "Capt'n," he said softly. "Come on. It ain't worth it. Let's cut the dust."

"Sí, el capitán," Javier whispered.

Miller tugged on his beard and smiled again. "Some other time, Ranger Jack." Watching them ride down Main Street, I started to go after them. Iowa Glen's strong hand stopped me.

"Don't press it, Jack," he said sternly. "Let it go."

Inside the office, I tossed the shotgun onto a cot, pulled the Colt from my holster and placed it on the desk. I knocked my hat to the floor and ran my fingers through my hair, inhaling deeply, and leaned back in the chair. My nerves and my stomach rattled. I picked up the .38, considered it briefly and rested the barrel on my right shoulder. Then I slid my forehead against my left palm, both elbows on the desk, and tried not to cry.

The door opened quickly. I sat up, cocked the Colt and almost blew Loren D. Lily's head off.

I didn't know the man at the time. He was a barrel-chested, fair-complected man with dark hair quickly graying, a neat mustache, and wore a tan corduroy coat and black Boss of the Plains. "Forgive me, Marshal," he said, raising his hands.

I told him to close the door, and as he did I eased down the hammer and placed the Colt on the desk again. Smiling, the man sat down in front of me, pulled a wallet from his coat pocket and handed me a business card.

"Loren D. Lily," I read. "Proprietor. Lily's Dry Goods. Caldwell, Kansas." He nodded and told me I could keep the card. I asked what brought him to Texas.

"The City Council asked me to come here," he said. "To seek you out, sir."

I picked my hat off the floor, put it on and waited for him to continue.

"I like what I've read about you, Marshal Mackinnon. Allow me to say that I regard most of what I read as pure poppycock, and I had some reservations about you, sir, if I may be blunt. But seeing you outside, facing that pack of rabid vermin, I changed my tune so that I agree with my fellow Councilmen, not to mention my ten-year-old Travis. Someone told me that shooting a handgun is more instinct than shooting long arms. Do you agree?"

"Never considered it."

"Well, sir. That sounds logical to me. I am a fair shot with a rifle or shotgun myself. In fact, last year I finished third runner-up at the Caldwell Thanksgiving Turkey Shoot, and we have some credible shootists in Caldwell, sir, as I'm sure you have heard."

I hadn't heard, but I didn't say nothing.

"Well, Marshal, when I came in here—rudely, I might add. Let me apologize again. Anyway, that Remington seemed to, let me see if I can get the words right, as I read this once in one of Robin Hunter's novels. Yes. It seemed a 'mere extension of your right arm.' " He smiled. "My son loves those cheap adventure tales, sir, makes me subscribe to the Wide Awake Library. I don't believe them, but I must say seeing you in action outside today made me think that perhaps much of what Mr. Hunter writes about is as honest as the Good Book."

My revolver was a Colt, and Robin was a woman. Instead of correcting Mr. Lily, I asked: "Is there a point to all this?"

Lily sat up straight. "Confound it, sir, I want to offer you a job."

"A job?"

"Yes. As town marshal of Caldwell, Kansas. I like your style. Shall we show our cards, Marshal? How much do you make in this wretched little town?"

"A hundred dollars," I lied.

"Is that all? Sir, I can offer you two hundred a month, plus eight bits for every arrest, five percent of every license fee collected in town, and you are free to make your own 'protection' fees from the gaming element. What say you, sir?"

He held out his hand. I hesitated.

"Marshal, are you one of those Texians who can't dare leave this miserable Lone Star State, even for two hundred a month?"

"No. Texas ain't my favorite place these days."

"Let's go to Caldwell, Kansas, Mr. Mackinnon. I assure you your stay will be rewarding."

Part Two, Kansas
1879–1880

Chapter Nine

In a lot of ways, Caldwell, Kansas, was pretty much the spitting image of Spanish Fort, Texas. Both were tinderbox towns on the cattle trail just a hop and a skip from the Indian Territory, serving forty-rod whiskey to anybody who hadn't took the pledge. Fact is, the reason I was here was because the last city marshal got himself fired for being drunk seven days a week.

Caldwell became incorporated as a third-class city on July 29, 1879. The railroad was coming, and when it hit town, folks figured Caldwell would be the next shipping point for the Texas herds. Right now, cowboys, drummers and owlhoots simply passed through. But the town was getting prepared. Mike Meagher opened up a saloon on Main Street. Big Mike had been the police chief up in Wichita. I wondered why Meagher wasn't wearing the marshal's badge till I learned he planned on running for mayor in the next election. Pretty soon, I figured out another reason. Big Mike was too smart to be Caldwell's lawman, though he dumbed up later and got hisself killed.

That winter passed slow. I collected my pay, tried to stay out of the snow, and passed time reading an old *Weekly Eye Opener* or even older *Hard Times*, which somebody had left behind in the room I rented off First Street. Later, I declared that the previous tenant left Dickens's book behind as a joke. *Hard Times* and Caldwell went together perfectly. I broke up a few fights in the saloons, arrested a drunk now and then and collected fines, taxes and those sorts of things. After rangering and marshaling in Texas, it was dull work. I liked it.

By spring, things started to pick up. Mr. Lily sent riders south, spreading the word to Texas drovers that Caldwell would be open for cattle business this season. That seemed to be wishful thinking because the tracks hadn't been laid much past Wellington. So I tried to get ready for real work, putting up my sign that made carrying firearms in the city proper subject to a fifty-dollar fine.

Loren D. Lily tore down the sign.

"Mr. Lily," I told him at a City Council meeting. "You're setting yourself up for bloodshed if you let a bunch of waddies walk the streets heeled. Even Dodge City has an ordinance against firearms."

The merchant smiled. "Good, then perhaps the Texicans will come to Caldwell instead. We don't want to run off business, Marshal, and the Texicans will put a lot of money in our pockets."

I nodded, and used my argument that had persuaded Mayor Boeke back in Texas. "You think about this. Everyone who wears a gun will pay fifty dollars to get out of jail. We'll confiscate that firearm and charge him to get it back. Ten dollars for a revolver or derringer, fifteen for a shotgun and twenty for a rifle. That sounds like a profitable venture to me."

"Nope," Lily said.

"We could make the fines higher."

"Nope. You're paid to keep the peace, Marshal. And your being a Texican will make things easier. You can better handle those halcyon waddies."

I ground my teeth, pursed my lips and quickly learned something about Kansans. They wanted the cattle business at all costs but didn't want the violence, never quite grasping—till it was too late—that you couldn't have it both ways.

"Well, I'll need some deputies once the herds start coming in."

Lily's head shook again. "The contract you signed doesn't call for the city hiring deputies. You are free to hire them, if you deem it necessary, but at your expense."

I searched for some friendly faces, but found none. Mayor Meagher looked down on me with a peculiar grin that seemed to say: *"You saddled this widow-maker, Mackinnon. Let's see if you can ride 'er."*

"All right, gentlemen," I said. "But you boys better start praying that the railroad's here before the first herd arrives. Else, we're gonna have us a shooting war that ain't nobody gonna stop."

The Cowley, Sumner and Fort Smith Railroad reached town on June 13, 1880. Times got a little hard for me. I was dragging a liquored-up cowboy out of the Red Light dance hall down North Chisholm Street when the boy begged me to let him walk. I sighed, relented, watched as the waddy—he couldn't have been out of his teens—pulled hisself up, wobbled over to a lamp post and begged me to shoot him dead.

I walked over to him, carved off a piece of tobacco and stuck it in my mouth.

"That gambler, he was cheatin' me," the cowboy said.

"They will do that," I replied. "Don't mean you can go shooting up the place. You're lucky I happened by. Mag Woods was about to blow your head off with a Greener."

I offered him a chaw. He looked at the tobacco, bent over and sprayed the street and boardwalk with regurgitated whiskey. Unfortunately, the boots Mr. Justin had made for me back in Spanish Fort didn't escape the carnage. Maybe I should have killed that boy when he asked me to.

The ramrod of the kid's outfit came by the next afternoon, paid the fine, and I let the waddy out of jail.

"I ought to go kill that cheatin' card shark," he mumbled.

I nodded. "Good. Then I'll arrest you and see you hang. Makes no never mind to me."

Frowning, the ramrod shoved the boy out of my office, then faced me. He was a big cuss with a dust-covered handlebar mustache that seesawed as he twisted his mouth and thought of something to say.

"That boy's a good kid," he said in a nasal twang. "If he says that gambler was cheatin', then it's the gospel. I don't like my boys gettin' hoorawed."

"I don't like my boots getting splattered. That boy of yours had so much whiskey he couldn't see straight. If the kid doesn't want to be cheated, he ought to stay in camp. So, you sold your herd?"

"Yep."

"Then take your boy and get out of town."

His mustache danced around a mite, and he swore underneath his breath as he turned to go. I made him stop at the door. He stared at me.

"I forgot something," I said. "There's an extra two bits to that fine."

"What for?"

"To get my boots cleaned."

He grunted, straightened and looked like he was about to charge, but finally he laughed and pitched a coin to the floor before walking outside.

I made my rounds, stopped for a bite to eat at a café on Avenue A and thought about that young cowboy's complaint. I didn't like cheaters. Back in my gambling days, I never dealt a dishonest hand. I sipped my Arbuckles and stewed. Tinhorns were bad for business. First of all, I didn't care too much for Mag Woods or her degenerate husband, and I didn't like that two-story blight that towered over the corner of North Chisholm and East Avenue A.

The Red Light wasn't far from the café, but I went to my office first. I had a .44-40 Colt holstered on my left hip, but the Woodses weren't no fans of law enforcement, so I pulled a confiscated Navy .36 from the drawer. This I shoved into my gunbelt. After putting on a frayed black frock coat, I walked to the establishment.

It was too early for George or Mag Woods, though the clock chimed twice. Jane, one of the upstairs girls, was making herself a gin and bitters when I walked in.

She was a small brunette in the wrong line of work. She downed her drink and gently fingered a slight bruise just below her left eye.

"Bad night?" I asked.

She shrugged and made her second drink—didn't even bother to ask if I was thirsty.

"You see what happened last night?" I asked.

"I was indisposed, Marshal Mackinnon."

"That cowhand said he was cheated."

"I wouldn't know nothing about that."

"You got a new faro dealer, right? What can you tell me about him?"

"Ask him yourself, Mackinnon." The neck of the gin bottle pointed behind me. I pushed the tail of my coat behind the holster and slowly turned.

Tenedore Keough looked more like a Charleston plantation owner than a cowtown gambler, with a white coat, frilly-front shirt, and straw hat. He sat dealing solitaire poker, smiling, and motioned me over. Dumbfounded, I dropped in the chair across from him, but the Navy Colt made sitting uncomfortable, so I drew the revolver and dropped it on the table between us. Some fellow picked that moment to drop in at the Red Light, and the next morning I read in the *Post* that

"City Marshal Jack Mackinnon and notorious gambler T. Keough were embroiled in a lethal game of faro yesterday at the Red Light. Eyewitnesses say that our heroic lawman pulled a deadly Colt's revolver and placed it on the table, daring the Texas butcher to 'make your play.' Two pairs of icy eyes locked with murderous intent, but Keough relented

and agreed to play clean games for the rest of his stay in our fair city."

Ten collected his cards and called: "Jane, sugar, would you kindly fetch a bottle of our best rye and two glasses for Marshal Mackinnon and myself."

Jane suggested that Ten do something else, so we went without refreshments.

"It's been a while, amigo," Ten said. "I reckon you have a million questions."

For months I had stayed awake at night, thinking, trying to remember what had happened at that jacal near the Red River. Finally, I had given up and written Tenedore Keough out of my life. And here he sat. And those memories flooded back.

You were my partner, my friend. And you let the captain almost kill me. Then I wake up on a cot with some sorry note from you. If it hadn't been for Iowa Glen, I'd probably be dead now—no thanks to you. Sure, you saved my life, but there's not a day that goes by that I don't think about those three Mexicans Captain Miller lynched. Questions? Yeah, I've got questions, and you better answer straight. What happened to Anse Deweese and Sergeant Thad? And, by everything holy, Ten, if you tell me you shot them, I'll kill you myself.

I thought this. Didn't say none of it, though.

"That cowboy who tried to shoot up this place last night says he was cheated," I said. "I want to make sure that wasn't the case."

Ten laughed. He leaned forward, pushed my coat away and tugged on the marshal's badge pinned to my shirt. "Ranger Jack, you've grown up a lot since we parted ways. You plan on running me out of town, Marshal?"

"Depends."

He shook his head. "The boy was full of John Barleycorn, Jack. Even if I cheat—and I don't—I wouldn't have to swindle him. He's worse at faro than Anse Deweese."

That hammered me. Spanish Fort, and all of the pain, raced back. I closed my eyes. Ten's cough brought me back to Caldwell. When I looked up, his smile had vanished and he sat sticking a handkerchief into his coat pocket, swearing at his bad lungs. We looked at each other. Ten fingered the barrel of the Navy and sighed.

"You ought to kill me, Jack. I wouldn't blame you. After I run out on you like I did."

"I don't care about that," I lied. "Tell me about Anse Deweese."

"I didn't shoot him. Didn't shoot Sergeant Thad, either. You know me better than that. But Captain Miller planned to stretch my neck. Best thing I could do, I figured, was to say out of Texas. Guess we got some catching up to do. You hungry?"

I wasn't, but said that sounded fine. Ten smiled, stuck his deck of cards into a coat pocket and I followed him outside. We went down Avenue A, turned right and walked up to a cute little frame house surrounded by a white picket fence. Ten held the door open for me. I took off my hat, stared at the fancy furniture in the parlor and looked at my reflection in a satin-framed mirror.

The door closed behind me. Ten said, "Honey, I'm home and brought a guest for supper."

Robin K. Hunter stepped out of the bedroom.

Chapter Ten

She could sing and churn out a tale, but Robin wasn't much of a cook. Not that I cared. I couldn't tell what we was eating and I plumb didn't care. I tried not to stare at her, and we passed through supper with idle chatter. Then Ten decided that our reunion called for champagne, so off he went to the nearest saloon to fetch a bottle. Robin and me retired to the parlor and made ourselves comfortable on a high-backed oak frame lounge.

Robin wore a two-piece yellow dress, trimmed with a blue bow, inset panel and stand-up collar. She looked beautiful. We talked about the weather for so long, it felt as if I was conversing with my dad back in South Carolina before yellow fever took him to Glory. Then we ran out of things to say. I sat there like a fence post. Finally, she offered that I looked good. I told her the same, and thought about our observations.

I reckoned we looked pretty good since we last laid eyes on one another more than a year ago. My last memory of Robin was of her fainted dead away in Iowa

Glen's arms. And me? I had been bleeding to death in a hotel room when she last saw me.

"How was St. Louis?" I asked after a spell.

"Fine," she said. "Ten came for me." She laughed. "I was surprised, to say the least." My heart sank. "Anyway, I had read that cheap novel that portrayed him as a cold-blooded killer, and Ten was in the news in the St. Louis papers, too. Well, when he came to my sister's house, I decided that maybe I could do some good." She patted my knee. "I'm writing again, Jack, for the Wide Awake Library. I'm hoping my books that portray him as a hero will help him, and you, make people forget about what happened in Texas. Maybe it'll stop the . . ."

She didn't have to finish. I had read about those bounty killers Ten left dead in Ogallala, too.

Ten barged through the door, waving his bottle, and when the cork popped out, it put a hole in the ceiling. Champagne spilled onto the floor, staining the rug. Ten just laughed. "Well," he said, "we're just renting the place." We had a toast, drank some tingly stuff, and Ten showed me his new revolver.

It was a double-action Colt Lightning, .38 caliber. with a three-and-a-half inch barrel.

"What do you think?"

"Make a good paperweight."

Laughing, he pulled back my frock coat and nodded at my Frontier Colt.

"Your taste hasn't changed. What was it Iowa Glen said? 'The long barrel comes in handy for accuracy and braining somebody.' "

Robin sighed. "Men and their toys," she commented and disappeared to make coffee.

"What happened to that matched set of Colts you borrowed from me?" I asked.

He shook his head. "Lost them. Aces and kings to three nines in Newton. That's why I prefer faro."

After a cup of coffee, I took my leave.

"I'll walk out with you," Robin said.

On the porch, I instinctively reached for her hand but came to my senses quickly enough to pull back. I opened the gate, and she leaned against the fence, smiling. She looked happy. I wanted to kiss her—I'll admit that—but didn't. We talked a while longer, then hugged. Ten stared at us through the window. I'm sure he didn't trust me. Couldn't blame him none.

"I hope we'll see you soon, Jack," she said.

"Me, too."

I walked away, feeling strange. There was no chance for Robin and me. Probably there never was, but I didn't know it for certain until then. A crowd had gathered in front of the Leland Hotel, and someone was talking up a storm. The Leland was one of the finest establishments in Kansas, three stories of brick with running water in each of its forty-six rooms. Mighty impressive. I pushed my way through the crowd to see a gent in a single-breasted corkscrew sack suit and brown derby. The Leland also had a barroom, and this fellow had obviously spent most of the day there.

He kissed a hardback card with gilt edges and a picture of a scantily clad female on it, and pulled a flask from his suit. Then he said:

> *"Come, bitter conduct, come, unsavoury guide,*
> *Thou desperate pilot, now at once run on*

The dashing rocks thy seasick weary barque!
Here's to my love."

The townsfolk cackled. The gent took a long pull from the flask, gagged and continued:

"O true apothecary,
Thy drugs are quick. Thus with a kiss I die."

Kissing the picture, he collapsed to his knees, let the breeze take the card down the boardwalk and expired. Everyone laughed. Except me. I kicked him in the ribs. His bloodshot eyes opened, and he greeted me with a curse.

"Folks are talking about building a opera house for plays and the like," I said. "But that's down the road a couple years or more. I suggest you come back then."

The would-be thespian climbed awkwardly to his feet and cursed me good and loud. A fellow could get roostered just from his breath. "Marshal," he said, "this is *Romeo and Juliet.* You know nothing about Shakespeare."

"I know I'm paid to keep the peace. And you're disturbing it."

He cussed me again. "Obviously, my friends," he told the crowd, "your marshal is heartless when it comes to true love."

Iowa Glen had been right. One of the reasons I preferred a long-barreled Colt was for pistol-whipping. Which is what I did then. I conked Romeo on the head pretty hard and run him out of town. Later, the newspaper editor asked me if I would like a job as theater critic.

Thinking back on it, that's about the only time I ever abused my power as a peace officer. Romeo didn't deserve no such thing. I was just mad. I regretted it. Still do.

So Robin wrote her book, Ten gambled and I marshaled. Ten and me would play billiards every now and then at the Leland. I kept trying to convince the Council to hire deputies, and Lily and his companions kept turning me down. A few more trail crews reached town, a few shot up The Last Chance Saloon just outside of town, and one drunken waddy managed to break his neck while racing down Main Street when his horse took a spill. Through it all, somehow, Caldwell didn't burn to the ground.

In late August, I found a copy of *Death Rivals; or Tenedore Keough's Secret Six* on my desk. When I read Robin's latest book, I went to the Moreland—Ten had moved from the Red Light—and found him drinking his morning rye.

"Have you read this?" I asked.

"Certainly. You look upset. Angry that Robin didn't include you in this one? Don't worry, Ranger Jack, she promises you'll return in our next adventure."

It wasn't funny. *Death Rivals* explained Captain Levi Miller's betrayal of Ten Keough, and outlined Ten's course of revenge. Now, all of this was Robin's sensational hogwash, but citing Miller's name seemed about as smart as smoking a pipe near an open powder keg.

The book even accused Miller and Javier Evaristo of murdering Anse Deweese and Sergeant Thad.

"Levi Miller will kill Robin for this," I said.

Ten tossed his empty shot glass aside. "Not if I kill him first," he said icily.

"You . . ." I stopped. I was about to say that if anything happened to Robin, Ten would answer to me. But that was dumb. Robin knew what she was doing. So did Ten. Me? I just hoped Captain Miller never read *Death Rivals*.

Besides, I had enough to worry about. Three trial crews had descended upon Caldwell. The cattle season was almost over without a murder or too much gunplay, but these cowboys weren't in a hurry to leave town. Business was good for Tenedore Keough and town merchants, and I kept busy myself. I disarmed two drunks from tearing the Leland apart, then went inside the Moreland Saloon with a shotgun to arrest a cowboy who had failed to pay for the boots, seersucker coat and collarless silk shirt he found at Loren D. Lily's.

"You ain't taking him in, lawdog," a cowboy informed me.

"He walks out, or I drag out what's left of him," I said. "You boys decide."

They stared more at the shotgun than at me. One scratched his palm with the hammer of his holstered Colt. I waited, all the while cursing Loren D. Lily to high heaven. Deputies. Why couldn't I get deputies?

The bartender picked that moment to clear his throat. "Boys," he said, "that's Ranger Jack Mackinnon. You'd better listen to him."

Them waddies, though, weren't literate types. They

had never heard of Ranger Jack. The barman tried again. "He's a friend of Ten Keough. They used to ride together. You shoot it out with Mackinnon, Ten Keough will track you down and shoot you down like dogs."

Fine. I had been reduced to Ten's "trusty companion" once more. Nor was I too pleased with the fact that the bartender was counting me out already. After all, I held a sawed-off Parker, and scatterguns were convincing persuaders in these affairs. Whatever, the thief walked out with me, and I locked him in a cell.

The foreman came in the next day, paid the fine, and I let the cowboy out of jail. He had sobered up but still threatened to kill me. "Your time's numbered, Ranger Jack," the foreman said. Threats didn't scare me, but I wished those cowboys would head back to Texas.

The door swung open while I was reading the *Commercial* over my cup of coffee. I blinked. It couldn't be, but there was no mistaking those green eyes, blond hair and wide smile. Sergeant Thaddeus James reached across the desk with his right hand. I spilled my Arbuckles, but didn't care as we shook hands and embraced.

"I ain't no ghost," Sergeant Thad said.

We started for the Moreland, but the cowboys were hanging out there, so I turned for the Leland instead. We found a corner table, drank a beer and Sergeant Thad told me how he had been in what the doctors called a coma for eight months. Still alive. I shook my head. Even Robin had made him a corpse in *Death Rivals*.

We ordered another beer. "You know who shot you?"

The smile faded. "We both know, Jack. Trouble is, we can't prove it." He sighed, and the beer suddenly tasted particularly bitter. "You know he's been kicked out of the Rangers, don't you?"

"Who? Miller?"

"Yep. And the reward he put up for Keough has been disallowed. He's still facin' a murder charge in Texas, but maybe without that reward, the bounty hunters will stay clear."

"Ten's here."

"Here! And you haven't arrested him?"

I sipped the beer. Truthfully, I never even thought about arresting Ten. "He's . . ." I studied this some more. "I'm just a city constable. He's not wanted in Caldwell." Seems I had heard that argument back in Dallas.

Sergeant Thad started to laugh, then frowned. "Well, I reckon we both know Ten didn't kill Anse Deweese either."

We had our third beers in silence. After wiping the foam off my mustache, I asked: "What brings you to Caldwell?"

"To see you. I rode back to Spanish Fort once I was able. Captain Miller had been run out of the Rangers by then. Anyway, Iowa Glen told me you were marshal in Caldwell, so here I am."

"Well, it's good to see you." I flagged the bartender for more beers.

"You might not think so," he said. "I was hopin' I might talk you into quittin' marshalin' and ridin' out with me. Maybe Keough would come with us."

"Where you headed?"

"New Mexico Territory."

I shrugged. "Never been there. You got a gold mine or something?"

"No. There was a little set-to in the Seven Rivers country. Miller and Evaristo made some noise. Last I heard, they were still hirin' out as paid killers. I aim to kill them."

I leaned back. "Thaddeus," I said, and that was likely the first and only time I ever called him anything but Sergeant Thad, "I can't help you there. Tracking a man down to kill him, no matter who he is, that just ain't my style."

He smiled. "I figured as much. I—"

Gunshots echoed somewhere in town, and a woman screamed. Someone yelled, *"Marshal! Come quick!"*

I stood up. "You interested in being a deputy?" I said, half-joking.

"Sure," Sergeant Thad answered quickly. "I'm short of funds these days. Besides, you once took orders from me. It's only fittin' that I take a few from you."

We shook on the deal. I wish to heaven he had turned me down.

Chapter Eleven

It was the same drunken cowboy I had hauled in before, the Bar K 5 troublemaker who had threatened to kill me. This time he and another waddy moseyed along Main Street shooting lamp posts until they came across a paint horse tethered in front of Lily's Dry Goods. Texas cowboys had a strong dislike for pintos, so one of the rogues shot the horse dead in its tracks.

Thad and me didn't have time to run to the office for scatterguns. We just went to the sound of the shooting, and when the two cowboys seen us, they holstered their guns and moved to the center of the street. Businesses suddenly closed. Down the street at Moreland Saloon, the Bar K 5 foreman and a half-dozen other cowhands had gathered out front to watch the show. Thad and me spread out, revolvers drawn.

I looked past the two cowboys in the street toward the Moreland. The batwing doors swung open, and I made out Ten's Boss of the Plains. He said something, though I couldn't hear the words. The foreman spun around, something flashed in the sun, and Ten left him spread-eagled on the street. The other waddies stepped back. Ten waved his Lightning, and slowly the cowboys un-buckled their gunbelts.

The second cowhand waiting for us turned at the sound of the commotion. When he faced Thad and me again, his pallor had changed to that of a dead man, not a drunk.

"Jake," he said pleadingly.

"Shut up, Rufus. We don't need nobody to back our play."

I stopped about ten yards in front of them, my Colt aiming at Jake's gut. Thad took another step to my right and waited.

"You're under arrest," I said.

Jake laughed. "Holster that gun of yourn, Marshal. Let's see how much sand you got."

Rufus had other thoughts. He unbuckled his gun, lifted his hands and moved out of the street, saying, "I got nothin' to do with this. I ain't armed. I ain't got—" He tripped over the dead pinto, and crawled onto the board-walk.

"I don't need him neither," Jake said. "Holster your gun, lawdog. Have your friend stay out of this. This is our dance."

There's a time for discretion. There's a time for bravado. And there's a time for shooting. I thumbed back the Colt's hammer, raised my arm just a tad, aimed quickly and shot Jake in the left thigh. He dropped with a scream.

Maybe it was the beer, or maybe I was just fed up. "How does it feel?" I hollered. Jake cursed and groaned, holding both hands against the gunshot wound. I walked, almost ran, over to him and let my right foot fly. The boot caught him right above the nose and sent him sprawling, unconscious, in the dust.

The Bar K 5 foreman slowly sat up in front of the Moreland. My job wasn't finished, so I walked toward him, feeling the blood rushing through my head. My ears felt like they had erupted in flames. The foreman shook his head, saw me and his mouth fell open when I put a bullet between his knees. He leaped back with a curse.

"You've worn out your welcome," I said, and looked up at the other Texans Ten had disarmed. "All of you." I cocked the .44-40 for emphasis. "If you're not out of town in an hour, I'll come a-killing."

I turned, walked to the unconscious cowboy and told Thad to lock him up and fetch a doctor. Next I faced Rufus. "How much money you got?" I asked.

The terrified cowboy pulled a purse from his vest pocket, peered inside and answered, "Three dollars."

"You're fined three dollars for disturbing the peace, and leave your weapons. Get your horse, drag the one you shot out of town and bury it or burn it. You savvy?"

"Yes sir."

"Does Jake own his horse?"

"Yes sir."

"Then bring it, saddled, and leave it tethered here for the owner of the one you boys killed."

"What about Jake?"

"Jake won't be needing a horse for a long spell."

Loren D. Lily opened the door and stepped out of the mercantile. I gave him a Texas-size haranguing, cussing him more than I done them Bar K 5 boys. I holstered my gun—maybe so I wouldn't shoot that rapscallion—and said, "The first thing tomorrow morning," I told him, "I'm putting up signs that prohibit the carrying of fire-arms in the city limits. If you touch one of those signs, I'll break your fingers."

"How much do I get paid?" Thad asked.

I laughed. Here he had just risked his life to help me out and hadn't even asked about payment until now, two days after I shot Jake Fargo. Things had quieted down since then. The Bar K 5 outfit left down, and Jake rested uncomfortably on one of the jail cell's ticky mattresses waiting on the circuit judge to get to town. I had charged him with everything but murder. Those signs were up, and although Loren D. Lily wasn't speaking to me, I had plenty of support, had even tacked up this headline from the *Post*:

MARSHAL ON THE WARPATH
RUNS WILD TEXICANS OUT OF OUR CITY
ONE COWBOY WOUNDED, JAILED
CITY LEADERS PRAISE MACKINNON
NO CONCEALED GUNS ALLOWED IN CITY LIMITS
EYEWITNESS REPORT OF THE SHOOTOUT

I told Thad I'd pay him fifty a month, and he agreed, so I went back to work replacing the firing pin on my Winchester rifle. Thad poured us coffee and stretched out in the rocking chair in front of the stove.

"What did Keough say about the concealed weapons ordinance?" he asked.

"He didn't say nothing. I told him the law applied to him."

Thad sipped the Arbuckles and sighed. "I reckon." He inhaled deeply again and let it out slow. I cocked the empty Winchester, pulled the trigger and placed it behind the desk, satisfied with my workmanship and waiting for Thad to continue. We wanted to talk about something.

"I owe you an apology, Jack," he said. "I guess that's one of the reasons I came here."

I waved him off. "What for? You don't—"

"Jack, I would have let Captain Miller beat you to death."

My stomach turned. I leaned back in the chair. Never had I been able to piece together exactly what happened at the Mexicans' place near the Red. Maybe I didn't want to know. For a long time, I had been bitter—not at the captain, whom I simply hated, but at Sergeant Thad and Ten for not throwing in with me. O'Brien and the others, well, sure I was disappointed, but I didn't expect them to side against Miller. Thad and Ten, though, they were my friends.

"What happened?" I asked uncertainly. "The last thing I remember was getting hammered by Miller, then waking up inside that jacal."

Nodding, Thad began. "Miller whupped the tar out of you. Keough and I watched, kinda thunderstruck. O'Brien just laughed. He was the captain's boy, sure enough. Last I heard, he was ridin' with Miller and Evaristo. Anyway, Keough suddenly whipped out those Colts, cold-cocked O'Brien and shot Miller's hat off his head. I wished he had aimed a tad lower. 'Next boy who moves gets himself killed!' Keough yells, and Miller turns around in a rage. But nobody does nothin'.

"Miller glares, tells Keough he's fired. 'I figured as much,' he says. 'But you lay another hand on Jack, and I'll bury you. Now mount your horse and you boys ride out.' They tossed O'Brien over his horse and left. Miller asked if I was comin'. I told him no, that I was sick of him and his killin', and told him I'd see that he was jailed for killin' that Mexican in Deweese's livery. Big mistake on my part. Anyhow, I stayed. We took you into that hovel, couldn't move you and the Mexicans didn't have a wagon. So we figured to ride into town, get help and come back. But we knew Miller would be after us. We figured it would be safer if I took the Mexicans to Spanish Fort. Keough would lead your horse away to the river, make it look as if you were with him and he'd leave it hobbled nearby in case somethin' happened to us. Then he'd hide out in the Nations a while."

Thad shook his head sadly. "Lookin' back on it, it was a most pitiful plan. I figured Miller would go after Keough. The last thing I remember, I was leadin' those Mexicans to Spanish Fort. I led them to their deaths instead. Almost led you there, too."

I stared at my Arbuckles for a spell. "Well," I said at last, "it don't matter. I'm alive. You're alive. And Captain Miller will get his in due time."

Thad cussed softly. "I aim to see to that myself," he said.

Robin took me out to supper at the Leland to celebrate my newfound status as hero of Caldwell. The editor of the *Post* dropped by just to shake my hand, and Major

Odum, who built the Leland, said supper was on him, even bought us a bottle of wine. To me, that was a major victory because Odum was probably the biggest cattle dealer in these parts, and the reason I was suddenly so popular was because I had made a stand against Texas cowboys.

We ate salmon, first time I had ever tasted the fish, and scalloped oysters. The salmon was mighty good, but I ain't got a thing to say about the oysters. Lot of folks love 'em. Lot of folks is sick in the head.

"How's Ten?" I asked. I hadn't seen him since I told him about the firearms ordinance, I guess, because I didn't want to have to fine or arrest him if I found him armed. And I knew he would been carrying that Lightning or some hideaway gun. He couldn't afford not to.

"We're not talking about Ten tonight," Robin informed me. She didn't look at me when she said this.

"Oh." There had been some complaints about raised voices at that nice little cottage Ten and Robin rented. I had ignored them. Ten Keough wasn't the easiest man to live with, I reckon, with his gambling and drinking and consumption, too. I heard tell he was on a lousy losing streak at the Moreland, and I knew first-hand that when things weren't going his way at the faro layout, he could be a disagreeable cuss.

It's funny, though. I had been deeply in love with Robin K. Hunter, and I was pretty sure she loved me— just not as much as she did Ten. But that had passed. Oh, I still had feelings for her, but this was just supper between friends, nothing romantic. We ate, drank wine, laughed, didn't talk about Ten and she promised to write a whole book about Marshal Mackinnon, the iron lawman of Caldwell. Then we strolled down the streets, before I stopped at my office to check on Thad.

I found him on the floor in a lake of blood, his head split open.

Robin gasped. Someone had written on the far wall in blood: U WANT FARGO, ITS YOUR LAST CHANCE

The door to the jail cells hung off its top hinge, and I knew the Bar K 5 boys, or some of them, had come back to down, busted out Jake Fargo and were waiting for me at The Last Chance Saloon. "Get a doctor," I told Robin and reached into the gun cabinet.

"You want Ten?" she asked.

"Get a doc!" I snapped, and she hurried down the street. I loaded a Remington-Whitmore double-barrel with buckshot, dropped a handful of extra shells into my coat pocket, drew my Colt revolver and put a sixth bullet into the chamber I kept empty for safety reasons. I also loaded a .45-60 Whitney-Kennedy repeater, though I didn't really care for the rifle, found Thad's bay gelding tethered out front, shoved the rifle in the scabbard and rode south.

The Last Chance Saloon was a log cabin on the north bank of Bluff Creek and had never been known for serving a more gentle clientele. A posse had burned the original building about six years back, and these days most cowboys preferred to do their drinking in the city limits.

A full moon had risen, lighting up the Kansas plains too much for my liking, so I swung a wide loop around the saloon and came up from Bluff Creek. I ground-reined the bay next to a two-seater in back of the saloon, pulled the heavy rifle and worked my way cautiously to the side of the cabin, shotgun in one hand, rifle in the other. One window was boarded up, and I couldn't see through the thick, dirty glass of the other, so I moved to the front of the cabin. The foreman sat on an overturned crate on the front porch. Inside, I heard the clinking of glass and chimes of a few sets of jingle-bob spurs.

I leaned the rifle against the cabin, brought the shotgun to my shoulder and thumbed back both hammers. A horse hobbled out front whinnied, and the bay answered. The Bar K 5 foreman heard, leaned forward and spun off the crate, drawing his revolver and yelling inside, "He's here, boys!"

I aimed low. The foreman, unfortunately, ducked as I let go with one barrel.

Smashing the nearest pane with the stock of the shotgun, I stepped back as bullets destroyed the rest of the window. I lined the coal-oil light hanging in the center of the saloon in my sights and pulled the trigger. The inside of the saloon exploded with flames. A bullet creased my left collarbone. Abandoning the shotgun, I grabbed the Whitney-Kennedy and made a fast beeline for the woodpile twenty yards away.

A cowboy stuck his head out of the front door. The Whitney-Kennedy roared. He yelped and flung himself aside. I sent another round pounding into the door for good measure, then stopped, my shoulder throbbing. A .45-60 kicks like a howitzer. The boys inside threw a few more shots at me before things quieted down. Inside, the flames spread.

"You boys throw out them guns!" I yelled. "And come out with your hands high!"

That, too, sounded like something Robin K. Hunter would have me say. Somebody answered with a curse.

"You boys can either burn up inside, or come out shooting with a posse. Or we end this peaceably. Death by fire or lead. Makes no never mind to me."

I was waiting for an answer when the revolver cocked behind me.

Chapter Twelve

My heart raced as I lowered the rifle to my knees. A voice behind me said mockingly, " 'Death by fire or lead.' Jack, you read too much."

Ten crawled up beside me, jacked a round into his Winchester carbine and braced the barrel against the woodpile.

By now, the flames leaped out the broken window in the front of The Last Chance and any horse out front that wasn't hobbled was running south through the Nations. The two hobbled horses screamed, fought and tried to flee the inferno. One fell on its side with a thud. Suddenly, a figure bolted through the door. I made out the white cloth wrapped around his leg and knew it was Jake Fargo. The Winchester flared as he fired rapidly from his hip, but his shots didn't come close to Ten and me.

Ten pulled the trigger. Jake Fargo fell dead.

After that, five hacking cowboys and one stunned bartender came out of the roaring saloon, hands up, faces blackened by smoke. Two Bar K 5 boys dragged the bodies of Fargo and the foreman away from the cabin, and two others freed the hobbled horses. One of those was a pretty fast thinker, because he swung into the saddle while Ten and me walked toward the ground and hit the trail at a high lope. Ten swore.

"Let him go," I said.

"Marshal," the bartender began, "I didn't have a thing to do with this. These boys come in, pistol-whipped me and—"

"Shut up," Ten told him. The barman obliged.

Squatting, I examined the man I hadn't meant to kill and the cowboy Ten had. "Fools," I said sharply, staring at my captives. "You had him broke out of jail and just a few yards from the Indian Territory. Once there, I couldn't touch you."

"Jake wanted revenge, Marshal," one of the cowboys said. "Didn't like you mistreatin' him like you did."

We heard the hoofbeats then, pounding, and saw the rider come racing in the moonlight. I jacked another round into the rifle. That cowboy who had escaped was coming back. Muttering an oath, I brought the heavy .45-60 up, but Ten stepped in front of me and whipped out his Lightning, which popped four times. The rider yelled and fell as the wide-eyed horse charged past us. I swung the Whitney-Kennedy around to cover the Bar K 5 boys, but they weren't doing a thing.

Ten holstered the Lightning, and we walked to the rider. He lay facedown in the dust. Ten shoved his boot under the dead man's stomach and rolled him over. The roof of The Last Chance collapsed, showering the night sky with sparks. My knees buckled. Ten let out a cry.

Thaddeus James stared up at us with sightless green eyes.

Sumner County Coroner's Inquest,
September 13, 1880
District Attorney, Lyttleton Fitch
Witness, John L. Mackinnon

(Q:) What is your title?

(A:) City marshal.

(Q:) So your jurisdiction falls only in the city?

(A:) I reckon so.

(Q:) But The Last Chance Saloon is out of the city limits, is it not, Marshal?

(A:) It is.

(Q:) So you had no authority there. This was a matter for the county sheriff. Am I correct?

(A:) I didn't pay much attention to that. A prisoner had escaped and Thad James—

(Judge Shinn addresses the witness to answer the question.)

(A:) It was outside my jurisdiction.

(Q:) Who killed Deputy James?

(A:) Tenedore Keough fired the shots, but I was about to. Thad came charging—

(Q:) That's all, Marshal. Tenedore Keough killed Deputy Marshal Thaddeus James. Had you deputized Mr. Keough?

(A:) No.

(Q:) So you had no jurisdiction as a city employee, and Mr. Keough had no authority. This was a heinous, lawless gunfight that left a business burned and three men dead.

(Defense attorney Flood objects. Judge Shinn sustains.)

(Q:) One more question, Marshal. After the carnage—

(Defense attorney Flood objects. Judge Shinn sustains.)

(Q:) After the gunplay, did you not tell Mr. Keough it might be better if he left town until, quote, "we clear this all up"?

(Judge Shinn instructs witness to answer the question.)

(A:) I did.

"Hero" is a fleeting thing. That extract from the inquest pretty much tells you how things went. What it doesn't mention is that District Attorney Fitch was Loren D. Lily's brother-in-law, and Mr. Lily was fed up with me. What the lawyers never let me say was how Ten Keough fell on his knees and bawled—the only time I ever saw him cry—over Thad James's body.

Thad came riding through the night like a madman into a hostile situation and didn't identify himself. I ain't saying it was Thad's fault. It was nobody's fault, just one of them things. The last person we expected to see riding a horse that night was Sergeant Thad, but he was always a Ranger. And in the end, the inquest left things alone, ruling that Thad James died an accidental death at the hands of Tenedore Keough, who was helping the city marshal try to apprehend an escaped prisoner.

They fired me, though.

I would have quit anyhow.

* * *

I walked Robin to the train depot. She was headed back to St. Louis before going on to New York City where she wanted to talk to her publisher about a touring play featuring the adventures of Ten Keough and Ranger Jack. In less than a year's time, the curtain would rise on *Best of the Bordermen* in Chicago, Louisville, Cincinnati, Pittsburgh, Buffalo, New York, Philadelphia, Baltimore, Washington and Richmond. I don't think it got one good review, but folks back East ate it up and made Robin K. Hunter a lot of money. Ten and me? We never saw a dime. A lot of people say that Robin just used us to further her own career. But they didn't know Robin.

She kissed me softly and got on board. I watched the train pull away until I couldn't even see the smoke in the distance. Then I bought a black quarter horse with one white stocking, used Thad's bay as a pack animal and left Caldwell. If I knew Ten, he'd be in Dodge City, so I rode northwest. I found his horse, however, in front of Big Bill's Medicine, a dugout on the Medicine River. Big Bill told me he'd give me a twenty-dollar gold piece if I could get Ten out of his establishment. "He's bad for business," he said.

Coughing harshly, Ten crushed out a cigarette and filled a beer mug with rye. He sat alone at the bar, which was nothing more than a plank stretched across two beer kegs. Business was bad. Ten was the only man there when I walked in.

"You're a long way from home, Marshal Mackinnon," Ten told me between gasps and drank half of his glass.

"I ain't a marshal anymore," I told him, and added a

lie, "I quit. Figured you'd be in Dodge by now. Thought I might tag along."

Ten shook his head. "If you were smart, Jack, you'd drop me now, ride out of here. I'll get you killed."

"Ten."

I waited till he looked at me. "I'm your friend."

He started to wave me off, but I pinned his right hand to the wood, spilling the rest of his drink. His hard eyes registered shock. "What happened to Thad ain't your fault," I said. "If you hadn't shot him, I was about to. Now you want to wallow around in self-pity, fine. But you owe Robin more. And me, too, I figure. I'm heading west. I'd like you to ride with me. But if you'd rather sit here and wait to die, that's your call, partner."

I mounted my horse, waited five minutes and was about to ride off when he walked through the door, shielding his eyes from the sinking sun, he had been inside for so long. He pulled himself into the saddle, saying, "I hear Las Vegas, New Mexico, is booming."

The shots came from behind us, steady but slow firing. Ten and me was breaking camp one morning in the grasslands along the Cimarron Cut-off. I looked at him.

"Buffalo hunter," he said.

"Shooting at what?" I said. "There hasn't been any buffalo in these parts in years."

"Well, it's none of our affair."

The big gun boomed again. I gave him my hard stare. Sighing, Ten pulled a deck of cards from his coat pocket, shuffled them and placed the deck on his saddle. "High card," he said. "You cut first."

I turned over the seven of spades. Ten laughed, and

cut the five of hearts. Swearing, he kicked out the camp-fire.

We left our animals at the foot of a sandy hill covered with scrub. Below, down the trail, I made out the roan horse and a man kneeling by a clump of green in an otherwise brown patch of land. Smoke puffed from the rifle, followed by the dull report of a long gun. Maybe nine hundred yards away, a train of six wagons sat motionless. An ox lay dead in its harness off the lead wagon, and a tiny figure worked desperately to cut the leather. The gunman fired again, and the man jerked and fell across the dead beast. Rifle shots banged from the wagon train, but the bullets only managed to kick up dust far from the sharpshooter. A baby's wail cut through the morning as the echoes of the last gunshots died.

I had brought Thad's Sharps rifle up the hill. Ten shook his head as I dropped to the ground, jammed a pair of sticks in the dirt and rested the heavy barrel in the "V" where the sticks crossed.

"Spot for me," I told Ten before he could argue.

I sighted the man through the telescope attached to the rifle and fired. "You're way high," Ten said, as I shoved another .50-caliber cartridge into the breech and set the trigger. I made out the gunman's brown beard through the scope as he turned his attention toward us, rapidly reloading his heavy rifle. The Sharps bruised my shoulder. The man screamed as the stock of his weapon exploded.

Ten laughed. "Scratch shot, Jack."

"I'll take it," I said.

Except the man had mounted his roan and loped toward us like a Ranger. I started to reload, but Ten yelled something about this being his territory, and before I knew it he had raced down the hill, mounted his horse and took off to meet that assassin. I read *Ivanhoe* many years later, and when I got to the part where those knights fought on horseback with those lances, I saw Tenedore Keough again, charging that killer, both of them firing away with six-shooters. When they were maybe twenty feet from each other, Ten fired his last shot and the man somersaulted over the back of his horse.

By the time I got down there, Ten sat in his saddle, wheezing, too tired to even reload his Lightning. I dismounted and looked at the man Ten had killed, shot in the throat, another "scratch shot."

Slowly, Ten straightened and swore. "You recognize him?" he asked.

I studied the corpse's bearded face and shook my head.

"Pretend he doesn't have a beard," Ten said.

I cussed myself as recognition came. The last time I had seen him had been in Texas right before Miller started pounding my brains out.

"O'Brien."

Chapter Thirteen

 F our Mexicans met us in front of the wagon train, all of them holding rifles and considering Ten and me with suspicion. A white-haired padre performed the last rites over the fellow O'Brien had killed while a woman clutching a shrieking baby dropped to her knees and cried. Pretty soon, a young woman knelt beside her, pulled the baby from the grieving widow's arms and handed the kid to a Mexican lady as old as Methuselah.

I studied the gents staring at us and said, "Howdy."

You would expect, seeing how Ten and me had just saved their hides, that we would have gotten a warmer welcome. The Mexicans talked among one another in Spanish, too fast for my ears to make out anything, and finally a tall, broad-chested man holding a Henry rifle stepped forward.

He wore the open-sided trousers favored by vaqueros, with gold braid and a scalloped leather seat, a pleated bib shirt and the expression of pure meanness. I mean to tell you his eyes were blacker than Satan's, and the dark mustache and black hat didn't add no friendliness to his countenance.

"What do you want, *gringos*?" he said.

I took off my Stetson and ran my fingers through my hair, perplexed at this lack of hospitality. Ten answered, "To see if you folks are all right. I'm Tenedore Keough, and this is Ranger Jack Mackinnon."

Apparently, the Wide Awake Library wasn't popular with this party. The mean fellow said: "Sergio Bayo is dead."

"So's the man who killed him," Ten added sharply.

Meanness nodded. "*Sí*. For this, we thank you. The rest of us are fine. You may go now, *gringos*, with your conscience clear."

About that time, a sweaty little man with a puffy face ran to us. He was an American, with a tan sack coat, ill-fitting high derby and a pair of silver spectacles hanging crookedly over a crooked, pointy nose. "Teodoro," the man said, "please!"

Meanness gave the newcomer a hard glare, shifted the Henry and said, as a way to excuse himself, I guess: "We must see to Sergio." The four Mexicans gathered around the crowd surrounding the dead man and the ox, looking more like vultures than pallbearers.

"I'm Judge Wilbur Pike," the man said, "of Santa Fe. We were on our way from Dodge City when that gunman started firing at us."

We shook hands, introduced ourselves—Pike had heard of us—and listened as the judge told us how they had come to Dodge for supplies and to pick up Delfina, the daughter of Don Valentín. Times were tough in New Mexico Territory, what with land grants being contested and more and more Anglos moving in, wanting land. Don Valentín was not a man of violence, but it seemed violence was coming to him. Pike ended his story with a heavy sigh. He had told us a lot, not even stopping to catch his breath, except who was Don Valentín, why he was coming all the way to Kansas for supplies or how come he didn't let his daughter take the train to Santa Fe. I reckon he figured we knew all that already.

"The man shooting was a former Texas Ranger named O'Brien," Ten said. "He had been riding with Levi Miller. Mean anything to you?"

Judge Pike shook his head. "I've heard of Miller, but his last known whereabouts were around Seven Rivers."

Ten wasn't even listening. He was looking at the young Mexican woman who had comforted Mrs. Sergio Bayo. Couldn't blame him, neither. Long, glistening black hair flew in the breeze, and the wind pressed her skirt against her legs as she stood slowly, head bowed, looking like an angel, listening to the priest.

"Perhaps we can accompany you to New Mexico," Ten said, looking back at the judge. "Be safer for all of us."

"You'll have to ask Don Valentín," the judge said. "And he'll tell you no."

Stepping out of an ambulance, Don Valentín smoothed his bolero jacket, a fancy corduroy job with conchos and leather trim. Teodoro handed him a flat-crown, stiff-brim black hat and whispered in Spanish. The old gent waved off Meanness and walked to the campfire, where we stood sipping coffee. He had short white hair and a neatly trimmed mustache, but his eyes were as hard as

Teodoro's and when he spoke, you couldn't mistake his authority.

"*Señor* Pike informs me that you wish to accompany us to Santa Fe," he said. "Although my family, vaqueros and their families thank you for your help, this I cannot allow."

"May I ask why?" Ten said. The girl walked up and stood beside the leathery don, who didn't seem pleased at her presence.

"I do not know you," the old man said. "I do not trust you."

"Judge Pike can vouch for us," Ten said. "We're former lawmen."

"Gunmen," the don corrected. "*Asesinos.* I, too, have heard of Ten Keough and Ranger Jack."

"Papa," the girl interjected. "These two helped us. We should—"

A sharp command and raised hand silenced her. "Is this what I send my daughter to school for? Is this what they teach you in St. Louis? To argue with your father in front of strangers? Be silent, Delfina. You have been East too long. Teodoro!"

Meanness appeared quickly and drug the young woman away, the two of them snipping at each other like coyotes fighting over the last morsel of meat. Don Valentín waited a minute, smoothing his mustache while regaining his composure, and said: "Permit me to ask. Why did you intervene on our behalf?"

This time Ten looked at me to answer. "We heard the shots," I said. "Saw that man firing at y'all, heard the baby crying, thought y'all needed help."

The don nodded. "For all you know, the man you

killed could have been in the right. That's what I mean when I say you are an *asesino*. I do not like men of violence. Good day, gentlemen. *Vaya con dios*."

We were escorted out of the camp. Judge Pike sighed and shook our hands. "Don Valentín is a hard man, but as I said, these are hard times. I'm sure you understand."

"Yeah," I lied.

"Well, I owe you two a debt. If you ever get to Santa Fe and need anything, please look me up."

So we left them, not speaking until I realized we were heading northeast. When I mentioned this to Ten, he nodded and said, "If all them New Mexicans are like that old don, I think I'll stay clear of that territory."

Anyhow, that's how we wound up in Dodge City after all.

I imagine you know all about Dodge City, so there's no need to paint a picture. Caldwell had the handle "The Border Queen," but Dodge was—still is—"Queen of the Cowtowns." Ten landed a job dealing faro in back of the Long Branch, and I went to work fixing and selling guns at F. C. Zimmermann's Hardware Store. Zimmermann was Prussian, and I had a hard time understanding him sometimes, but I liked him. Ten did good himself at the Long Branch, and we probably would have stayed in Dodge—longer at least—if we hadn't met Noble Ward.

It was a Friday night in November, with a norther moving a lot of real estate. The bartender at the Long Branch said Ten had gone to the Varieties Saloon for a poker game and had asked for me to meet him there. *Great,* I thought, pulled up the collar of my mackinaw and went looking for him. I was south of the deadline (where anything went, firearms included), a block or so from the Varieties, when the girl screamed.

Habit caused me to reach for my Colt, only the revolver wasn't there. Living and working in Dodge City proper, I had stopped carrying my pistol mainly because I couldn't afford the hundred-dollar fine. I looked down the alley and saw some drunk in a buffalo robe who had pinned a girl's arm against the warped planks of an abandoned saloon.

"You gonna give me a kiss, missy," the man said.

The girl turned away from him, tightened her lips and closed her eyes. The drunk laughed. I found a rotted two-by-four some scavenger had left behind and stormed down the alley. That fellow was so in his cups he didn't even hear me till I shouted something. He let the girl go, turned around and I smashed his face—well, the two-by-four got smashed more.

I cussed my bad luck as he wiped his bloody nose, then I buried my fist into his lousy coat. Didn't even bother him. A backhand sent me sailing across the alley, and the drunk charged after me. I imagine I would have suffered a pretty good beating then—that brute was six-foot-four and shaped like a rain barrel—if he hadn't tripped. I rolled out of the way. His head slammed into a trash can. A cat screeched, bottles and cans rattled and the drunk lay stretched out cold.

The girl hadn't moved. She stood staring as I picked myself off the ground, brushed away the dirt and walked over. She shivered, so I let her have my coat. I never will forget those blond curls and that dress she wore. None of them belonged south of the deadline.

"You shouldn't be here," I said.

"I know. Will you take me home?" It had been years since I had heard a Southern accent that refined, that musical. I didn't ask her name, and she didn't say anything till we got to the Western Hotel.

"My father and I are staying here," she said in a voice as sweet as molasses. "Thank you for your kindness . . ."

"Jack Mackinnon," I told her.

She smiled. I watched as she entered the hotel, still wearing my mackinaw. I had thought about asking for it, but didn't want to seem rude. So I stood on the boardwalk, getting colder every second, until I chalked up my lost coat to Southern chivalry and went home to warm up.

Ten and me was eating dinner at the Delmonico, and he was complaining about me not finding him the night before. He droned on and on, but just like that he stopped. I realized he was staring so I turned to see a tall man with a reddish-brown mustache and goatee standing next to the blond girl from the alley. She wasn't wearing my coat.

The man introduced themselves as Noble Ward and his daughter, Mollie, and asked if they could join us. We made room in a hurry.

Ward had sky-blue eyes just like Mollie, and they fell on me as he absently found a cigar in his coat. "My daughter says you came to her aid last night. As her father, I thank you."

Ten looked at me bewildered-like. "What happened?"

I shrugged. Mollie looked away. Noble Ward answered, "Some ruffian accosted her, pulled her into the alley between Zimmermann's and the drugstore. If it weren't for Mr. McKay . . ."

Well, there wasn't no alley between Zimmermann's and the drugstore. Mollie Ward needed to improve her lying, but her father hadn't caught her yet. Noble Ward gave us each a cigar; I would have preferred my mackinaw.

"It's Mackinnon," Ten said. "Not McKay. This is Jack Mackinnon. I'm Tenedore Keough." He tipped his hat. "At your service, ma'am."

She smiled, and I got a strange notion: Mollie Ward had been on her way to the Varieties last night to see Ten. They knew each other. I could see that in their eyes. Noble Ward interrupted my thoughts.

"Not *the* Ten Keough and Jack Mackinnon!"

"Only ones I know," I said. It come out kinda arrogant, but I hadn't meant it that way. Noble Ward didn't mind, or notice.

"I should have known," he said. He flagged the waitress down for our check, insisted on paying for our dinner and taking us to the Alhambra Saloon for a whiskey and a game of billiards. Mollie went back to the Western Hotel. After Noble Ward had whipped us good on the billiard table, he bought us another drink and asked if we wanted a job.

"I own a ranch in New Mexico Territory," he said. "Actually, I own a great deal more. A store. Mining interest. A few saloons." He laughed. "Some say I own more than a few senators and can buy and sell governors."

"What kind of job?" Ten asked.

"I need men," he said, "such as yourselves. Good men

who can handle themselves. Men I can trust. A war's brewing in the territory, again, and I need protection for my daughter."

I was about to tell him no when he added, "Two hundred dollars a month and found."

Ten said, "We'll take it, Mr. Ward."

I could have shot him. After Ward left, I stared at my pard while the bartender poured us another whiskey, compliments of Mr. Noble Ward.

"Thought you wanted nothing to do with New Mexico," I said.

"I'm fickle."

"Yeah, you just want to get closer to Mollie." When he laughed, I added angrily, "I ain't blind, Ten."

"You don't have to come, Jack."

I didn't either. But I went. We was pards.

Part Three, New Mexico Territory
1880–1881

Chapter Fourteen

Noble Ward's Crown Ranch lay in a valley dotted
with juniper, piñon and cholla. The main building was a
long adobe and looked more like a fortress than somebody's home. Stone corrals, solid lean-tos of cedar, cook
shed, barn, privies and other buildings surrounded the
ranch yard. All you had to do was run up a Yankee flag
in the middle of the parade ground and you'd have yourself an Army post.

Ten and me were invited into Ward's office, where
the rancher filled three tumblers with French brandy. It
was nine o'clock. In the morning. I waved mine off and
stared out the big window. A couple of fellows unloaded
the buckboard that had been waiting for us at the Lamy
depot. About a half-dozen or so sat on the bunkhouse
porch out of the wind, just loitering about. One or two
had the nerve to stare at Mollie as she gave the cook
orders for supper. Not a one of them looked like a cowboy.

"You have a nice ranch," Ten said.

115

"It's taken years of hard work," Ward commented. "I aim to keep it, but I need more. I have government contracts to supply Fort Union up north and Fort Stanton to the south with beef. Two herds will be on their way from Texas this summer. I need all the land I can get. The trouble is, Don Valentín, my neighbor, won't sell. He hates all Americans."

"Lease the land," I said.

Noble Ward looked at me like I was a leper. "Valentín won't do any business with me. I opened a store in his miserable town over the hills. Do you know what he did? He went to Dodge City, got Judge Pike of Santa Fe to go in as a partner, and has opened his own store. As I said, he hates Americans."

"Pike's an American," I said.

Ward gave me a cold look. Ten stared at me too, telling me without speaking to keep my trap shut. I didn't pay no heed.

"You don't have to lease with him. Seems to me it would be better to lease land near those forts."

Ward shot down the rest of his brandy and ignored my comment. "I'm afraid Don Valentín will start trouble. I'd like to do this all legally, peacefully, but it's best to be careful when you're a man of my stature. I don't want this to turn into another Lincoln County War."

Ten asked, "So what do we do?"

"Perhaps you'll just sit around the ranch and draw my money. Whenever my daughter takes a notion to ride to Santa Fe, I'd like you to escort her." He looked like a weasel when he smiled. "I'm sure you'd both like that. And, if trouble comes, I expect you to earn your money. Agreed?"

Before we could answer, someone knocked on the door. Ten and me turned as Ward said, "Come in." The door swung open, spurs jingled and a tall man with a gray beard and grayer eyes ducked inside. He wore a buckskin coat and a brace of nickel-plated Smith & Wesson Second Model Russians with checkered ivory grips. My stomach leaped to my throat, and I warmed my palm with the butt of my holstered Colt.

"Gentlemen," Ward said, "I believe you both know Leviticus Miller."

Miller laughed when he saw us, hooked his thumbs in his gunbelt and shook his head. "Boys," he said, "it's been a long time. Ten Keough and Ranger Jack. My soul be condemned to Hades."

It already is, I thought, but I couldn't speak. Ten looked just as stunned as me. If we had thought about it, been just a hair quicker to react, we could have shot the man dead then and been done with the matter.

"He work for you, Mr. Ward?" Ten asked, though his eyes stayed locked on Miller and his hand hovered over his Lightning.

"Yes. In fact, he's my foreman, so to speak. You'll take orders from him or me. Understood?"

We walked out without speaking. Miller snickered and said, "Don't worry, boys. I ain't one to hold a grudge."

But I was.

Ten stopped when Mollie called for him on the porch. He told me he'd catch up, so I went to the corral to saddle our horses. Javier Evaristo spotted me from the bunkhouse. There was no mistaking that eye patch and cigar. But he didn't do nothing.

I had my black saddled and had just thrown the blanket over Ten's bay when he ducked through the rails and told me he was staying.

"Why?"

He shrugged. For once, he couldn't look me in the eye. "Two hundred a month is a right smart amount of money," he said. "Besides, this dry climate might be good for my lungs. And Ward hasn't asked us to kill anyone yet."

"He will."

Ten cussed. "That old Mexican? We've met him, remember? If you ask me, his reputation smells like a dead steer in July."

"So does Noble Ward's."

I pitched the saddle blanket to the dust, slapped the horse's rear and asked Ten to open the gate. After mounting the black, I told Ten, "Miller will kill you."

"Or I'll kill him, if it comes to that. Maybe we'll do the world a favor and kill each other. But if you ride out of here, everyone around will call you a coward."

"I can live with that."

Ten sighed and held out his hand as I rode past. I ignored him.

Two miles later, I reined up. From what I had learned in my short stay in the territory, northwest, under that snow-capped peak, sat Santa Fe. I could find a job there, or ride the rails out of the territory. I could head north to the gold fields in the mountains, maybe on to Colorado, be done with Tenedore Keough, Leviticus Miller and Noble Ward lock, stock and barrel. But I thought about them dying Yankees back in Florence, South Carolina, thought about my vow to help those in need. I should warn Don Valentín of Ward's intentions. He deserved to know he would be going up against the likes of Levi Miller. Northeast were the foothills, and beyond them a tiny village called Zavala that served as headquarters for the Valentín Land Grant. That's the way I turned.

Two miles south of Zavala, I found the Valentín *rancho*, tethered my horse at the corral and noticed the excitement. Vaqueros had butchered a cow and were preparing to cook it, while a handful of women massaged the buckets of blood with their feet and hands, like them wine-making grape-stompers I heard about. I was so perplexed at this activity, I didn't hear the person come up behind me.

"They will fry the blood with onions and peppers, *Señor* Mackinnon. It is quite delicious."

Delfina Valentín Zavala smiled and brushed the bangs from her eyes as I turned.

"I'll have to take your word for it, ma'am," I said, then remembered my manners and removed my hat.

"Call me Delfina."

I started to tell her to call me Jack, when I got this funny feeling. Looking back at the vaqueros and women, I saw one man standing away from the butchering, frowning, looking as mean as ever.

"Your husband might not care for that," I said.

"*¡Esposo!; ¿Quién?*" She laughed when she spotted Meanness. "Teodoro's my brother. *Venga.* I'm sure you are calling upon my father."

The *rancho* was a whole different setup than Ward's spread. We walked through heavy wooden gates to a

Johnny D. Boggs

flagstone *placita*. "This is my home, *Señor* Mackinnon," she said, and I quickly added, "Call me Jack."

Smiling, she pointed out the chapel and trade room. Cooks moved around the kitchen next to the granary, and the smell of the fresh tortillas and beans reminded me that I hadn't eaten. We walked past a well, and Delfina pointed inside a big room with a hand-adzed floor. "We will have a *fandago* tonight, Jack," she said, "then have Mass to celebrate. Perhaps you can stay, no?"

"I'd like that," I said. "What's the party for?"

She laughed again. "It's Christmas Eve."

I followed her down a narrow passage to the rear *placita* and another series of rooms. She opened a door, motioned me inside and I waited in an office. On the far wall hung a giant portrait of a handsome Mexican man and a beautiful woman standing in front of an ornate adobe church. The woman had raven hair and the delicate nose and dark, haunting eyes of Delfina.

"My daughter looks very much like her mother," Don Valentín said, closing the door and motioning me to a high-backed leather chair in front of his white pine, beautifully engraved desk. "I married very late in life but was blessed with beautiful children."

"Your wife is very beautiful, too."

"Was. She has been dead for ten years."

The door opened, and Delfina entered. Don Valentín's ears burned but he kept his tongue in check. The old Mexican filled two glasses with wine and sat behind the desk. Our glasses clinked, and we drank. Delfina waited silently at the door.

"I do not believe you have come for Christmas Mass," he said.

I placed the wineglass on his desk, careful not to spill any. "Noble Ward offered Ten and me a job," I said. I went on to tell him that Levi Miller was working for Ward, that Miller was a notorious gunman, that O'Brien had been riding with Miller and that I figured Miller and Ward were behind the ambush on the Cimarron Cut-off.

"So you abandoned your partner?"

"Yes." That was tough to say.

"You expect higher wages from me, is that right?"

I waited, letting his words sink in. "No." I shook my head. "That ain't it at all. I just wanted to warn you. You deserve that much. Ward's a powerful man, and Miller will kill for spite. Ward wants your land. I figure he'll do anything to get it."

Don Valentín smiled. "So I am to believe that you left your friend to join my side? Or are you a spy?"

"Papa!" Delfina cried.

"Silence!" The don's icy eyes fell on me.

I rose. "I ain't a hired killer, Don. For Noble Ward— or for you."

Valentín stopped me at the door. I waited. He asked Delfina to leave, adding an uncharacteristic *"por favor."* When she had gone, he slowly rose, taking his wineglass in his right hand and holding some paper-bound novel in the left, and walked to the portrait, staring at his dead wife's image. He addressed me, but never took his eyes off the painting.

"Perhaps I am mistaken about your motives. But hear me out. Many years ago, I was much like yourself. Perhaps I am no different from Noble Ward either. *Capitán-General* Don Diego de Vargas granted this land to my grandfather's grandfather's grandfather in 1695, but it wasn't a gift. To be honest, we took this land from the Indians and for the past thirty years, *norteamericanos* have tried to take it from me. Noble Ward is simply the latest. Anyway, as I said, I was much like yourself. I used a gun. I killed men. Men foolish enough to try to take my land paid with their lives. One night, ten years ago, raiders came at night. Alicia, my wife, was killed in this senseless brawl. In madness, I charged and tackled a rider, strangled him with my bare hands. When I looked up, I saw Delfina, and I shall never forget that terrified expression upon her beautiful face. She was only twelve then. This heartbreaking look was directed at me. I looked back down and realized that the man I killed was not one of the raiders, but Bartoloméo Marcelo, my best vaquero who had ridden in to help. Do you know what it feels like to kill—to murder—a friend?"

I remembered Sergeant Thad, but said nothing.

"So what, Jack Mackinnon, has bloodshed accomplished? What will our sins reap for us other than the keys to Hades? I am but an old man now. I do not need hired killers. I have a good friend in Judge Pike. If Noble Ward wishes to take my land, he will have to fight Judge Pike, too, and Ward is too smart for that. I appreciate your concern, but I must ask you to leave my land and never return. For my daughter's sake."

His last statement caught me off-guard. I stood chewing on this for a second and he handed me the book. I saw the worn cover of *Ranger Glory*. Don Valentín's smile held sadness. "I send my daughter to school, expecting her to return reading the classics. She fills her head with this nonsense. I have enough trouble controlling my son, Teodoro. If I permitted you to stay, I'm afraid I would lose control of my family. And I do not wish my daughter to marry a killer such as yourself. Good night, *Señor* Mackinnon. *Adiós*."

I was more than a tad perplexed as I found my way through the *placitas* and grabbed the reins to my horse. Marriage? Delfina and me had scarcely traded a dozen words. The saddle creaked as I wearily pulled myself up. Delfina stood beside the heavy gates, waiting.

"My father is wrong about you," she said softly.

I didn't say nothing. "I went to the tack room next to his office and listened," she explained. "You are not a killer."

She didn't add any insight to that marriage stuff, though.

"Don't believe all them stories you read about Ten and me," I said.

"I don't. But I can see in your eyes that you are a man of peace, a good man."

I backed the black away, tipped my hat and said, "Take care of yourself, Delfina Valentín Zavala."

"*Vaya con dios*, Ranger Jack Mackinnon."

Chapter Fifteen

I wintered that year in E-Town and Cimarron, riding as messenger on the stagecoach run through the Palisades. This was high mountain country, and it might have been the prettiest I ever seen if not for the snow. That was the coldest I ever been in my life. Can't say I earned my money; nobody in his right mind would think about holding up a stage in that weather.

Lonesome Elmer was my driver, a good cuss who sang on the whole miserable run. The only song in his repertoire was "Jimmy Crack Corn." If my fingers hadn't been so stiff, if the wind hadn't drowned out most of those not-musical strains, I expect I would have strangled Lonesome Elmer sometime in January.

Mostly, I kept to myself, wondering what I'd do come spring. I thought a lot about the old don and Delfina, but the only time Robin crossed my mind was in February when Lonesome Elmer tossed a copy of the latest Wide Awake Library volume, *Ranger Jack; or, The Marshal of Iron*. There I stood with my hair to my shoulders and a flowing goatee, six-gun raised over my head, standing back-to-back with another gent with his gun raised while six or seven spectators got ready to watch us duel as the moon rose behind them.

I never read that book. Smiling, I handed Lonesome Elmer the novel and said, "Looks like I need a haircut."

"Ain't you gonna read it?"

"Naw. You read it for me."

"You knowed I can't read."

I didn't read *Ranger Jack* because I didn't like what I had become. John Lindsay Mackinnon, the Florence County farmer who had made a vow to help those in need. John Lindsay Mackinnon, the gunman, *asesino*. How many men had I killed? Two Fyfe brothers, two men in Spanish Fort, the Bar K 5 foreman. I wasn't exactly sure how many horse thieves. It's a bad thing when you can't count the number of lives you've taken. Most folks can, easy. Zero. Don Valentín had been right. I had told him I didn't hire out, but that wasn't true. At Spanish Fort, Caldwell and now here, I had a job because of my skill with a gun, my reputation for using one.

Whiskey didn't help much, neither.

Lonesome Elmer and me went to Lambert's in Cimarron for the rye and the stove one February afternoon. I stopped when I recognized the brand on the three horses tethered out front. It was a king's crown, Noble Ward's brand. "You comin'?" Lonesome Elmer asked.

I nodded, unbuttoned my coat, felt the butt of my Colt, and walked to the bar.

Three fellows I didn't recognize stood there, passing a whiskey bottle and idle chatter, laughing, keeping to themselves. We took a spot beside them, and Henri poured our first drinks on the house. I considered the three men for a minute before relaxing. Truthfully, I thought maybe they had come to kill me, but that wasn't the case. I was sure of that. For all Ten Keough and Noble Ward knew, Jack Mackinnon was back in South Carolina slopping the hogs.

"Still don't see why you won't read that book," Lonesome Elmer commented. "If somebody was to write a book about me, I'd read it, after I learned how."

"Maybe I can't read."

"You can read. I seen you with that Cimarron *News*." He flagged Henri over and bought us a couple of beers.

I started to reply when one of the men to our left snorted and told one of his saddle pals, "Did you see the look on that Mexican gal, Wade? What was her name, Daphne?"

The middle man laughed. "No, it was Del-something. I tell you I thought she might drop dead in the middle of that dirty store."

The last man said: "She was almost buried when we tore down them walls, sure enough. How long you reckon it'll be till it's safe to go back?"

The fellow nearest me answered: "Miller said wait a couple of months. Easy money, pards. Hey . . ."

The man was staring at me.

"There any decent women in this town?"

The man called Wade added, "Decent to look at, he means."

Lonesome Elmer answered for me and looked around for Henri. The man had disappeared, so Elmer climbed over the bar and refilled our mugs. Henri had gone to get the sheriff, though none of us knew it at the time.

He later told a reporter for the *News* that "Mackinnon's eyes had assassination in them."

"Where you boys from?" Lonesome Elmer asked, pouring them beer, too.

"Down south," Wade said. "Punching cattle for Noble Ward."

"Punching pretty Mexican gals, too," the first man added.

I smashed his face with the whiskey bottle. Wade stepped forward, but I had drawn the Colt and cracked his head open with the long barrel. The last man reached for a holstered .44 Dance, one of those relics from the War that looked like the offspring of a Navy Colt and Dragoon. I glanced quickly at the men on the floor. Wade was out cold, and the other held both hands against his bloody face. I cocked the Colt, lined up the sight on the last man's top vest button, watched as he brought the Dance up and thumbed back the hammer. I didn't move, couldn't move, not even pull the trigger.

All I had to do was squeeze my finger, but Don Valentín's words blasted through my ears: *Asesinos. I, too, have heard of Ten Keough and Ranger Jack.* The man leveled the cap-and-ball revolver. I wondered what it felt like to die.

His face disappeared, and he dropped to the floor in a bloody heap. Slowly, my muscles relaxed, and I lowered my Colt, saw Lonesome Elmer behind the bar, chest heaving, hands clutching like a club the shotgun Henri kept behind the bar, staring at me like I was a crazy man. Maybe I was. He cussed and took a long pull on the nearest bottle.

"What was you waitin' for, Jack? That boy woulda

killed you!" He drank greedily again, wiped his lips and stared at the three men. "What was that all about?" he asked in a befogged way.

I shook my head slowly, dropped the unfired Colt on the bar and walked into the cold.

I rode past the jacals and worn adobe structures, saw Ten's bay tethered in front of the Crown Mercantile, a two-story building with a gabled roof and adobe fence, went on past the cantina, the blacksmith's shop, a café with a barking dog out front, past the abandoned office of the *alcalde* with a jail in back that couldn't hold a two-legged cat, dodged the chickens in the street and reined up in front of the Zavala Store on the far end of town.

Miller's men had been thorough. They had pulled down the west wall and ridden through the store on horseback until the roof collapsed. But the store remained open for business. Bales of hay stood as a temporary wall, and a canvas tarp flapped in the wind as a serviceable roof. Behind the corral and privies, Mexicans worked on constructing new blocks of adobe. I swung from the saddle and walked to the door. Teodoro, hands clenched so tight against that old Henry rifle that his knuckles whitened, blocked my way.

"My father told you never to return here," he said.

"I want to see your sister," I said.

Neither one of us moved. His black eyes locked on me with savage intensity. After two minutes, he mumbled something in Spanish and stepped aside.

I had always known Delfina was beautiful, but as she stood behind a dusty counter, stacking sacks of rice that sold for six cents a pound, I realized there was a quiet dignity to her, more so than anyone else I had ever known. I stared—gawked is more like it—and took off my hat. She must have felt my presence because she stopped, frozen for a few seconds, before turning slowly. A bruise had formed under her left eye, and her lips were swollen. Neither diminished her beauty or dignity.

"Delfina," I said.

"Jack," said she, and we left it like that for a moment. She shrugged. "We had some visitors."

"I know. I ran into them in Cimarron."

"Did you . . . ?"

"No. They're in jail. I talked the sheriff into holding them until you and your father press charges, if you want. Can you identify them?"

"Sí." There was a bitterness, a hard edge to her simple reply. Couldn't blame her none. "They did not bother to wear masks."

"I doubt if they'll testify against Ward or Miller, but you can at least lock them up."

She looked past me. I backed up and saw Don Valentín standing in the doorway, a leather quirt in his right hand. I guess we both thought he was about to use the whip on me.

"I told you never to set foot on my land again," he said.

"I'm riding, Don Valentín. I just wanted to make sure Delfina was all right and to tell you where you can find the three men who done this."

"To kill them?"

"To lock them up. They're in jail now."

I nodded at Delfina and brushed past the old Mexican,

put my foot into my stirrup and stopped. The don had called out my name, not gunman or *asesino* or Ranger Jack. It sounded more respectful. "*Señor* Mackinnon, would you be interested in working for me?"

I stepped away from the black. "I thought you don't hire gunmen, Don."

He smiled, revealing straight white teeth. "I am not blind, John. You are not wearing a gun."

We leaned against the well in the front *placita,* looking at the twinkling stars in a black New Mexico sky. Delfina laughed as I shivered. "Ranger Jack," she said softly, "it is not even cold."

Maybe I still hadn't thawed out from the winter. Somewhere in the distance, a coyote started singing, and others quickly joined in. Delfina took a deep breath. "There are days," she said softly, "when I wish I were a thousand miles from here. But at nights, there is so much tranquility, so much of God here. Listen to the owl!"

I didn't hear anything but the coyotes. I stepped closer to her. Her black eyes filled with humor. "My brother and father suggest I keep a healthy distance from you. Teodoro would like an excuse to shoot you, even though Papa would disown him."

"How come you don't have a beau?"

"I spent the past ten years in St. Louis, Ranger Jack."

"I find it hard to believe you didn't have a mess of boys chasing after you there."

"Sneaking boys into a convent is not an easy thing."

I laughed. "But you could sneak in half-dime novels."

She blushed. "Ranger Jack was my hero. He was

much more sympathetic yet courageous than Achilles or Saint Paul."

I blushed. "Now, Ten Keough's supposed to be the hero in those books, Delfina. Ranger Jack is the 'trusty companion.' "

The owl hooted. "Permit me to ask," she said. "Why is it that you do not have a beau?"

Robin K. Hunter appeared before me, but she wasn't the same. The blue eyes couldn't mesmerize. The touch of her hand couldn't chill. I shrugged and moved even closer to Delfina.

"You cannot kiss me tonight, John Mackinnon," she said and stifled a giggle.

"Why not?"

"Because Teodoro is watching from the *granero*."

Chapter Sixteen

I had the makings of becoming a top clerk. Delfina told me that as we unloaded supplies for the store. A wagon with the Crown brand painted on its side squeaked down the street, the driver snickering as he passed us. Delfina spit and fired off a few Spanish unpleasantries that she hadn't learned in a convent. She pointed to a flour barrel I had just unloaded.

"You see that?" she said angrily. "If you were to go to the Crown Mercantile, it would cost you four dollars. But if I or anyone of my heritage tried to buy it, it would cost eight dollars. When Papa tried to buy our food and supplies in Santa Fe, our wagons were raided before they reached home. That is why Papa was forced to open the store."

"Ward wants this land."

"It's not just the land, Jack. He would prefer to see my people driven south of the border."

"All Americans ain't like that, Delfina."

She threw a can of lard at me. "I am an American,

too, Jack!" Her eyes filled with tears, and she pulled her long hair. "I'm just as much an American as you or Noble Ward!" She turned and ran inside the store, sobbing.

She called it "just an emotional day," said she was sorry, but I did most of the apologizing. The next day, everything was back to normal, more or less. Workers threw up the first adobe blocks to replace the destroyed wall, and crowds of Mexicans from all across the county came to our store for supplies. Since my Spanish wasn't *muy bueno,* Delfina relegated me to the outside, smiling, tipping my hat at the ladies and complimenting their babies. Reckon I wasn't such a top hand as a store clerk after all.

Don Valentín arrived in an Indiana Piano Box buggy pulled by a roan mare. The top was up, the black leather already covered with dust. After setting the brake and putting his quirt aside, the old gentleman stepped down and shook my hand. He wore a linen duster over a black suit.

"Business is good, no?" he asked.

"Business is good, yes. Where are you bound?"

"Santa Fe," he said. "Judge Pike has arranged an interview with the governor. I'll swear out a complaint against those fiends who attacked Delfina and the store. Noble Ward made a major mistake. My store also serves as the post office. This is a federal offense."

He drew a nickel-framed case with an embossed leather cover, opened it up and offered me a cigar. I bit off an end, spit out the piece and saw the don shaking his head, holding a cigar clip in his other hand. Laughing, he returned the clip and case and patted my shoulder.

"Tell Delfina good-bye for me," he said. "I should be back in a few days."

I fired up the cigar and took a seat on a rocking chair out front, watching the buggy disappear in the dust as Don Valentín made his way to the capital. He never made it. A vaquero hunting coyotes found the carriage overturned and the horse killed a few miles from Santa Fe. Inside an abandoned mission nearby, he discovered the old man hanging from a cottonwood *viga*.

The canopy-topped surrey clipping its way down the cobblestone streets toward mission looked much finer than Don Valentín's old buggy. The driver reined up in front of me, while the gent sitting next to him shifted a Winchester carbine. In back sat Noble and Mollie Ward, both dressed for mourning.

A crowd the size of some counties back East gathered for the funeral Mass, way too many people to fit in the little chapel at the *rancho*. So the funeral was held in Santa Fe, where the governor, lawmakers and many more could pay their respects. Even then, a hundred or so folks had to wait on the steps or in the churchyard. I probably could have sat with Delfina, but I really hadn't been accepted by Teodoro or many vaqueros, so I waited under a juniper. The last person I had expected to see stepped out of the surrey, telling his daughter to wait.

"Hello, Mackinnon," Ward said. He offered his hand. I resisted the urge to break his fingers.

"You're not welcome here, Ward. Light a shuck for home."

Ward shook his head. "I've come to pay my respects, to offer my services to that poor girl and her brother. I may have had my differences with Don Valentín, but I didn't want to see him dead."

I responded with a quick curse, louder than I meant, that caused a few heads to turn on the stone steps of the mission. The gunman in the surrey cocked the Winchester. More heads turned. Noble Ward held up his left hand and called the gunman's name. "It's all right," he said. "Besides, Mr. Mackinnon isn't wearing a gun."

"Nor was Don Valentín."

"I had nothing to do with that. Now if you'll excuse me . . ."

"Go right ahead, Ward. But I guarantee you one thing. If you walk up those steps, there will be a double funeral in Santa Fe this morning." I glanced at the driver and gunman. "Maybe even triple or . . ." I couldn't think of the word, so I let it lie.

Footsteps and heavy breathing sounded behind me. Judge Pike stepped past me and shook Ward's hand. "Mr. Ward," he said. "The family appreciates your sympathy, but, sir, it might be best if you left town. Many of the don's men hold you responsible. . . ."

"I can prove my whereabouts and was nowhere near that mission where that old man was murdered. Senator Curtis was with me that entire day, sir!"

"I mean no offense, but . . ." Pike shrugged.

Some vaqueros moved from the churchyard toward us. The Winchester-toting gunman suddenly lost his confidence. So did Noble Ward. "Very well, Judge," he said. "If you would please offer condolences from Mollie and myself, I would appreciate it."

After they had gone, I took my anger out on Pike. "You know he did it! He may not have put the rope around the don's neck, but . . ."

"You'll never prove it, son. Not in a court of law."

"Fine law!"

"Then do something about it, Jack. Run for county sheriff next election. But whatever you do, make sure you do it within the letter of the law, the way Don Valentín would have wanted it."

He started to go, but I asked him to stop.

"Judge," I said. "You once said if I needed anything, to ask you."

He scratched his nose, waited.

"Well," I said. "I'm about to ask."

Delfina stayed in her bedroom the morning after we returned from Santa Fe, so I went to the store alone. Before leaving the *rancho*, I opened my carpetbag and pulled out the long-barreled Colt, shell belt and holster. Blocking Don Valentín from my mind, I dropped five brass cartridges, sticky with corroded leather, into the cylinder, closed the chamber gate and slid the revolver into the holster.

The wall and roof were up. I half-expected Miller's men to tear the place apart while we were gone, but that would have been too obvious. Still, the door was open, so I entered slowly.

Ten Keough sat on rickety chair in front of a cracker barrel, twirling a Piccadilly parasol made of garnet satin over his black Stetson. "Y'all sell many of these things?" he asked, and tossed it over his head. "Been a long time, amigo."

I closed the door, pulled down the shade and moved in front of him. Slowly, I pushed back my coat, hooking the tail behind the holster that held the .44-40. Ten shook his head and popped a cracker into his mouth. "I heard Ranger Jack was going around undressed these days," he said after swallowing.

"Old habits."

Ten wiped his mouth with his left hand. "Word is the Mexican population is talking you up for county sheriff," he said. "Lot of other law-abiding folks, too. I guess they believe what they read in *Ranger Jack*." He laughed. " '*The Marshal of Iron.*' "

"Election's a long time away," I said.

"Yeah. You might not live that long. I've heard tell of a five-hundred-dollar bounty on your scalp."

"You aim to collect?"

He popped another cracker in his mouth. "Two guys waiting across the street are."

I didn't look away. I wasn't that green. My eyes stayed on Ten's. I cursed him, cussed our friendship. "You pathetic son of a—" The scraping chair legs cut off my insult. He put his right hand on the Lightning's butt. "Where were you when that crazy hangman Evaristo killed the don? And don't tell me it wasn't him." I went on before he could respond: "You're taking blood money because of some strumpet with blond curls. You can't stand your weakness so you'll side with a scalawag like Noble Ward or a butcher like Levi Miller. And to think I used to ride with you. Keough, you're worse than Ward or Miller. You ain't even worth the air your pathetic lungs—"

His right hand flew, but the revolver stayed holstered.

The knuckles smacked my face, stinging my jaw, cutting the corner of my lips. I tasted blood, saw Ten's eyes glaring. He shook as he spoke:

"And what of you, Mackinnon? You're a backstabbing cheat, or have you forgotten about your little dalliance with Robin? Maybe you have. After all, now that you've got that little Mexican gal cooing over you, her father feeding the worms and you in fine shape to get part of five hundred thousand acres—"

My backhand sent him crashing against the counter, spilling a candy jar over calico. He came up savagely, jerking the Lightning as my hand reached for the Colt. A violent burst of coughing stopped him. Ten fell on his knees and hands, head down, spitting out blood and saliva, working hard to breathe. I saw him then as he really was, a dying little man scared to die.

The .44-40 slid back into my holster, and I reached for him to help him up. "No!" he said angrily, and waved me off, a movement that caused him to lose his balance and fall to the floor. The spell subsided and he rolled over, resting his back against the counter, still wheezing, his face void of color.

Finally, in a raspy voice, he said, "Those two men will kill you, Jack. I mean it."

"Then why are you here?" I asked.

"Miller sent me in case they ain't up to snuff."

He pulled himself up without my help, wobbled and collapsed into the chair. "You think you can take me, Jack?" he asked, and hooked his right thumb near the .38 revolver.

A five-year-old who had never held a gun before could have killed Tenedore Keough then. "I don't think we'll have to find out, Ten," I said. "Those two men outside'll probably do the job."

I drew the Colt, pulled the hammer to half-cock, thumbed open the chamber gate and clicked the cylinder once. With my left hand, I drew a cartridge from the shell belt and dropped the bullet into the empty chamber. I thumbed the gate closed, pulled the Colt to full-cock, slowly lowered the hammer and eased the Colt into the holster.

"So long, Keough," I said and walked toward the door.

The chair legs scraped again. I didn't remember anything else.

Chapter Seventeen

The knot above my left ear felt as big as the cylinder of a Navy Colt, but much more tender. Delfina knelt beside me, pressing a damp cloth where Ten had hammered me. I sat up. Dizziness sent me back down. I lay like that for a minute, eyes closed, blood pounding the head wound. "What happened?" I asked, as if she knew. She had discovered me on the floor, covered with the cloth brushes, blacking daubers and turkey-feather dusters I knocked off the table on my way to oblivion.

"Jack," she said softly, "there are two dead men in the street."

Nausea passed. With Delfina's help, I rose, used the wall for support and peered through the window. One man leaned against a water trough, his white shirt stained crimson, head tilted at an awkward angle. A gaunt dog sniffed his boots. In the center of the street lay another man, his black coat covered with dust, right hand reaching for the Remington revolver just out of his grasp, pain and surprise etched on his face for eternity.

Neither man was Ten.

"*Señor* Keough killed them both," Delfina said, "then disappeared inside *la canting*. The man of Noble Ward, the ugly one with the eye patch, he says if anyone touches those two dead men, he will kill them. He says they will lay on the street and rot, that maybe the smell will drive us off this land. Teodoro is gone, Jack, as are our vaqueros. No one in town will bury those men. They are afraid. Jack . . ."

She swallowed, brushed a tear from her cheek. "Jack," she said again, "the man in black is one of those who came to the store, who tore down the wall. You said they were in jail in Cimarron."

My eyes locked on the face of the man in the street. Delfina was right. It was the man called Wade. I figured his two friends would be somewhere around. Set free on bail or broken out of jail, it didn't matter. Noble Ward had won again. Maybe not, I thought again. Wade was dead.

I rested my hand on the butt of the Colt. Delfina's eyes glanced downward, but she said nothing. "Wait here," I told her and stepped outside.

Javier Evaristo and two of Ward's riders rested underneath the covered porch in front of the old constable's office, across from the cantina, probably waiting for Ten to come outside. The one-eyed hangman smiled when he saw me. *"Hombre,"* he said, "it is good to see you again."

I walked toward them. Evaristo's companions took a couple of steps back, flanking him. My right hand tightened on the Colt. I stopped in front of them, never taking my eyes off Javier.

"Get those two bodies out of here," I said.

"No." Evaristo clucked his tongue. "Keough killed them. He can come out and bury them if he has the nerve."

"They're your men," I said. "You bury them. Or I'll bury you."

The man on the left laughed. "All three of us, Ranger Jack?"

"You first, Javier," I said. "I'll drill a hole in your gut, maybe break your spine. You'll be a long time dying."

The batwing doors to the cantina squeaked open, and I knew Ten stood in the doorway, waiting, backing my play once again. Evaristo's black eye widened. Slowly, he reached inside his serape and withdrew a cigar holder. He opened it, found a cheroot and stuck it in his mouth. "Take Wade and Brown to the cemetery," he said softly.

"But—"

"Do it!"

When they had collected the corpses and drifted back toward the Crown Mercantile, I went inside the cantina.

Ten slumped in a high-back chair at a table near the door, trying to pour rye into a beer mug but mostly drenching the table and floor with forty-rod whiskey. Blood rimmed his pale eyes, and his face was void of color. He looked like Death.

"Three-to-one ain't good odds, Jack," he said. "Javier would have killed you dead."

"Evaristo's a gutless coward," I said, "unless Miller is with him. What about those two you killed?"

He shrugged. "Don't expect I'll be collecting any more money from Noble Ward." He drained his whiskey, winked and exploded in a storm of coughs, overturning the table, dropping to his knees, spraying flecks of blood onto the dust-covered floor.

I fell beside him, pulled him close. He looked up weakly, gasping for air, and I leaned him onto the floor. "Ten?" My voice trembled with fear. He tried to say something, but I couldn't understand his faint, hoarse whisper. I turned to the saloonkeeper, a pockmarked man named Manuel Joven.

"Help me get him out of here," I said.

The Mexican shook his head and backed away, scared of the consumption. "No. No can help."

I swore as Joven fled outside.

"Jack." Ten's voice sounded clear. I looked down at him, forced a smile.

"You'd better get a priest," he said.

Lando Garcia had run a tonsorial parlor in La Mesilla before coming to work for Don Valentín in 1869. A short, squat man with black hair like a buffalo, he was the closest thing to a doctor between Zavala and Santa Fe. He came from the bedroom at the *rancho* and poured himself a glass of the don's wine. Delfina and I waited until he had drained one glass and half of another.

"I have given him a syrup of tamarack bark and the roots of dandelion and spikenard," he said. "Give him cream and brandy when he can take something. That is all we can do, except wait."

"How bad is he?" I asked.

"He will not get out of that bed."

My head dropped. I felt Delfina's hand on my shoulder. "He should have been buried long ago," Garcia said.

"The saloons, smoke, whiskey . . . none is healthy. It is as if he wished to die."

"Can I see him?"

"He is sleeping. You should let him rest."

I sat in the don's chair later that evening, sipping his brandy. Delfina came in.

"You have not eaten," she said.

"Not hungry."

"You are wearing a gun again."

She hadn't mentioned this before, though she had seen the revolver at the store. She walked closer and set a tray of tortillas, beans and *pollo asado* on the desk. The .44-40 Colt remained holstered on my hip.

"My father—"

"Is dead." I cut her off. The harshness of my words stunned her. I sighed, rose and said softly, "Delfina, everything's changed. Just because I'm wearing a gun doesn't make me an evil man. You know that. I think Don Valentín did also. I'm trying this without bloodshed, his way, but this county is about to explode."

"I know," she said. "I just wish . . ."

I wrapped my arms around her, pulled her close. We stood like that until Teodoro's voice broke the silence.

"Keep your *pistola, gringo*," he said. "We have need of it now. They have killed Bolivar Viento."

The letter from Judge Pike arrived shortly after we buried Bolivar Viento, a vaquero found shot to death near the foothills bordering Noble Ward's range. I crumpled the paper and tossed it into the cook fire on the placita. *"Mr. Mackinnon,"* the note had read.

I am sorry to inform you that I could not help you secure the position you seek. I strongly suggest you run for county sheriff. With many regrets, I remain your obt. servant,
Judge Wilbur C. Pike.

I found Teodoro loading the Henry rifle.

"Where are you going?" I said, though I knew the answer.

"Bolivar was my friend," he said. "He should not have been shot like that, alone, like a *lobo*. Noble Ward will pay for Bolivar's death and my father's as well."

"That's just what Ward wants you to do. That state senator is back on his place, visiting. You go riding in there, and if they don't kill you, you'll be handing over your ranch to Ward."

"And what is it that you plan, Ranger Jack?" Sarcasm turned his voice icy. "Sit and wait till all of us are shot from the saddle? There is no U.S. marshal in the territory now, the governor is trying to clean up the stink in Lincoln County and Noble Ward owns the county sheriff. I will not die like my pacifist father. If you do not have the stomach for this, go crawl into the bed with your lunger friend and die."

As he passed me, I whirled, whipped the Colt revolver up and down and smashed the back of his head. The Henry rifle clattered on the flagstone, and I managed to catch Teodoro before he fell, too. I dragged his unconscious body inside the study and stepped outside—into Delfina's arms.

"Lock up your brother until he cools off," I said.

"Where are you going?"

"To Santa Fe. I'm still trying to do this your father's way."

For two days, I tried to see the governor. For two days, I collected splinters in the seat of my pants, kept shaking my boots to keep my feet from falling asleep. Judge Pike had left town on business. My trip had failed miserably.

I sat alone in the dining room at the Exchange Hotel, eating green chili stew despite the warmth of May, staring outside at the gas streetlights, wondering what to do. A man cleared his voice. A handsome man with a thick mustache and beard, both meticulously groomed, short hair and penetrating eyes, he was dressed in a suit that would cost some men six months's wages. Two men flanked him. If they were bodyguards, they were overdressed. The man held out his hand and smiled.

"John L. Mackinnon, I presume."

"Yes sir."

"I'm Lew Wallace."

I stared across the table as the territorial governor pulled out a flimsy paperback novel titled *Ranger Jack*. "I apologize for not seeing you sooner," he said, "but my mind has been preoccupied." He tapped a long index finger on the cover of Robin K. Hunter's book. "This really isn't my taste, you understand, but Pat Garrett recommended that I read it. He speaks highly of you, as does William F. Cody and Senator Coke of Texas."

I had never met Garrett, the Lincoln County sheriff and soon-to-be slayer of Billy the Kid—or Buffalo Bill or Senator Coke for that matter—so I kept quiet. And I could understand why Wallace wasn't a fan of Robin's cheap novels. An accomplished writer himself, Wallace had just had a lengthy novel published in New York last winter. Perhaps you've read it: *Ben-Hur: A Tale of the Christ.* What I couldn't figure out, as I sat at a table with Wallace and his two companions, introduced as Mac-Veagh and Ritch, was what this was all about.

"Mr. Mackinnon," Wallace finally said, "I have resigned as territorial governor and shall be appointed minister to Turkey. I depart New Mexico at month's end. I do not, however, wish to leave my successor with two cauldrons from Hades, one in Lincoln County, the other along the Don Valentín Grant. You have a reputation, a strong one, in Texas, New York and Washington. People know of 'Ranger Jack' and what he stands for, and I cannot attribute of all this to these five-penny dreadfuls. When I saw your card at my office, it was like a godsend."

"You've lost me, Governor."

He smiled again. "We need peace in this territory, son. Don Valentín was a man of peace. We need a peacekeeper. We need a man like 'Ranger Jack.' "

This perplexed me some. "Sir," I said, "I had asked Judge Pike to see if he could get me a commission as a deputy federal marshal."

"Pike?" Wallace stroked his long beard.

MacVeagh said, "He's a judge here in the city, Governor."

Something started gnawing on my gut. "Governor," I said, "Don Valentín was on his way to see you when he was murdered. I was told he had an interview arranged with you."

Wallace shook his head. "I would remember that," he said. "I admired and respected the late Don Valentín."

"What's your deal with Noble Ward?"

Wallace's eyes flared. He didn't like being interrogated, not this way. "The rancher may have had some influence with my predecessor, he may be connected with others in our government, but I assure you, Mr. Ward and I have no deal."

MacVeagh cackled. "You see, Lew, Mackinnon here isn't afraid of the territorial governor. He's just what we need."

Relaxing, Wallace nodded, smiled, offered me a cigar. "Let us get to the point, Mr. Mackinnon. Wayne MacVeagh would like to offer you a job."

My eyes brightened. "As deputy marshal?"

The three men burst out laughing.

Chapter Eighteen

The bald little clerk in the tweed vest and sleeve garters grumbled when I entered the office south of the Plaza. He removed his spectacles and rose from his chair, beginning, "As I told you yesterday, Judge Pike is—"

I slammed the Colt across his forehead and sent him crashing to the floor. Footsteps sounded behind the door across from the desk. I covered the distance in four steps, kicked the door off its hinges and saw Judge Wilbur C. Pike clawing his way through the window. My right hand gripped his coat. He squealed like a sow as I sent him tumbling over his desk, showering the floor with cigars that spilled from their wooden case.

Before he could move, I straddled his body and pressed the barrel of the Colt against his nose. He stared up at me through broken eyeglasses. Sweat poured down his face like rainwater. The hammer of the .44-40 clicked menacingly. Judge Pike began to cry.

"You two-bit, pettifogging cheat," I said. "You set Don Valentín up to be murdered."

149

"No, I—"

"Governor Wallace says there was no interview arranged. And that deputy marshal's commission you couldn't get for me . . ." I jerked the legal notice from my coat pocket and tossed it on his quivering chest.

"Here's what I think," I continued. "Noble Ward owns you. He told you to befriend the don, get the family to trust you. Then he told you to tell the don about a meeting with Governor Wallace. You sent the letter, knowing Miller's men would be waiting for him on the road. That makes you an accessory to murder. So now, I figure the plan is for you to drop in on Teodoro and Delfina and have them sign some papers the next time you're at the ranch. They trust you. They'll just sign all five hundred thousand acres to Noble Ward. Am I right?"

"No, Jack, I swear—"

"I'm going to kill you, Judge."

There's a moment in everyone's life, I reckon, when you learn more about yourself than you'd care to know. I could kill, could shoot Pike in cold blood. My finger tightened on the trigger.

"Wait!" Pike screamed. "Please, don't. Listen, it's not like you think. I . . . I . . . ." He bellowed uncontrollably. I lowered the hammer gently and holstered the Colt, lifted Pike by the coat and tossed him into his chair.

He licked his lips. "I . . . It's not . . . Don Valentín was my friend, honestly. We went into business together to open that store." Pike paused long enough to mop off his sweaty brow. "I ran into Noble Ward in Dodge City. He said a lot of things could happen on the Santa Fe Trail. Remember when we first met? The gunman shooting at the wagon train. Later, Ward came to my office, asked if I remembered what happened on the Cimarron Cut-Off. I swear to you, Jack, that I had no idea they were going to kill Don Valentín!"

I drew the Colt, leveled the barrel.

"Please!"

No, I didn't kill him. I thought of Delfina, of my conversation with Governor Wallace. Jack Mackinnon, peacekeeper. Not Jack Mackinnon, murderer. Slowly, I lowered the Colt again, my hand trembling now, and sank into the chair in front of Pike's desk. The judge buried his face in his hands and crumpled onto the desk, bawling like a newborn calf. My eyes fell on the overturned wooden cigar box near his head. A vague memory cleared.

I swore. "Sit up, Judge," I said sharply.

I was too late. The Zavala Store lay in smoldering ruins when I returned. My heart jumped as I swung from the saddle and ran inside the building. Delfina wasn't inside.

Saloonkeeper Manuel Joven met me outside, his face ashen, lips trembling. "They came, Ranger Jack!" he said. *"Muchos norteamericanos!"*

Except for Joven, the whole town seemed abandoned, even the Crown Mercantile. They'd be waiting for me at Ward's ranch, knowing I would come.

"Delfina?" I cried.

"Sí."

"Yes, what? Is she all right?"

"Yo no se. El padre de la iglesia la llevó a su casa. Un vaquero fue a buscar a Teodoro. Eso es todo lo que

sé." He wiped his eyes and added in English, "Ranger Jack, they also shot my dog."

I galloped to the *rancho* and stormed inside until I found Lando Garcia. Actually, he found me and pinned my arms against the granary's wall. I tried to fight him but couldn't. For a short man, a barber at that, he was all muscle.

"She is alive," he said firmly. "A few broken ribs, I think, a concussion. She swallowed much smoke, but she will live."

I broke away, inhaled deeply and felt relief. "Where is she?" I asked.

He led me to her bedroom. She looked so fragile as I knelt at her bedside and felt tears warm my face. We were so close to ending this—what had Governor Wallace called it?—this cauldron from Hades. I shouldn't have left her, should have done it Teodoro's way. I gripped her hand, buried my face in the bedsheets and cried.

"Jack?" Her voice seemed so far away.

I straightened kissed her hand, brushed hair from her eyes and sat beside her. She tried to smile, but pain turned it quickly into a frown.

"I sent Teodoro south," she said, "to stay out of trouble. Did you see the governor?"

She drifted back to sleep before I could answer. Tears rolled off my face, darkening the bedsheets. Leaning forward, I whispered into Delfina's ear: "You are the gentlest, nicest, most wonderful woman I have ever met. You deserve better than me, Delfina. Please forgive me for what I have to do."

I rose, inhaled deeply and exhaled, and walked away,

knowing I would fail Don Valentín, fail Delfina. Her voice surprised me, and I turned around in front of the door.

"Ranger Jack is my hero," she said. "He shall always be my hero."

"I love you." I don't know. The words just blurted out before I could think. She didn't answer. She had fallen asleep again.

Outside, a frowning Lando Garcia handed me a badge. "This," he said, "the *padre* found pinned on the blouse of *la señorita.*" I stared at the circled star cut from a peso. Sickness rolled through my stomach. My fist tightened over the badge stamped *"Captain, Texas Rangers, Company G,"* and I rocked with rage and nausea. Leviticus Miller had left it as his calling card.

I stopped in Ten's room on my way out, sat in the chair by his bed, watched the sheets barely rise with his breath. His eyes opened, but I had no idea if he heard me. "Ten," I whispered, "I need you to do me a favor. Keep this for me." I slid a piece of paper into his cold, deathlike hand. The last will and testament of John Lindsay Mackinnon. Ten made no response other than lick his lips and close his eyes. I left him there, found a sawed-off shotgun and .44-40 Winchester carbine, loaded them, mounted my horse and left the *rancho.*

Justice? Revenge? Both? I don't know. I guess it's not for us to decide. Don Valentín wouldn't be proud of me on this day. He had been right all along. I was Jack Mackinnon, *asesino.* I rode to the Ward ranch, knowing I would have to kill Levi Miller, Javier Evaristo, maybe even Noble Ward himself. I rode there knowing that I, too, would die.

*   *   *

The wind picked up as my horse climbed the juniper-covered hill. From the top, I could make out the Ward ranch, but the mountains in the distant became a vague outline in the dust. I glanced behind me, saw a rider following me. Teodoro? No, he would bring as many vaqueros with him as possible. I gripped the stock of the Winchester before recognition hit like a mule's hind legs.

"This ain't none of your affair!" I yelled at Tenedore Keough when he was close enough to hear.

He didn't answer until he had reined up beside me, then wiped his lips with a shirtsleeve and said weakly, "You're wrong, Jack." Hatless, he looked like a corpse in a saddle. His boots were on the wrong feet, his bib-front shirt barely tucked in and the Lightning .38 shoved in the waistband. I have often wondered how he managed to crawl out of bed, mount a horse and gallop his way to catch up with me. You can say a lot of bad things about Ten Keough, but he had more strength and courage than most men I've known.

"You should be in bed, Ten."

"For what? To die?" He fought back a cough, groaned, took a deep breath. "If I'm going to die, it'll be with you, amigo." He smiled then. "Let's give Robin something else to write about."

I don't know how he managed to stay in the saddle as we rode down the hill and across the valley to the adobe ranch headquarters. A half-dozen men stepped out of the bunkhouse after we tethered our mounts and walked to Noble Ward's house. I tossed Ten the Winchester and shotgun, figuring I would need both hands free. Five other men came from the barn. The door to the main house opened, and Noble Ward stepped onto the porch, followed by Levi Miller. Another man timidly stood in the doorway, hands trembling, constantly licking his lips. Senator Curtis, I guessed. A handy witness for Noble Ward—if Curtis didn't get killed in the gunfight. I searched the compound for Javier Evaristo. Finally, his blackened face appeared as he rounded the corner of the main house, his serape whipping in the wind.

"Let's do this right," I told Ten. "Say 'I do.' "

"I do."

"You're deputized."

Evaristo pulled out his cigar case. Miller tugged on his beard. Noble Ward stepped forward and placed his hands on both hips.

"You're trespassing."

I slowly opened my coat, tugged on the first paper and handed it to the rancher. "That's a warrant for two of your riders for destruction of the Zavala Store and inter-ference with mail delivery."

Ward let the wind carry the paper away, where it lodged in a piñon branch. "Pike signed that warrant, that craven . . ."

I handed him the other warrant. "This one charges Javier Evaristo with the murder of Don Valentín."

"That's impossible," Miller said. "Javier was with me when that fine old Mexican was lynched. I'll swear to it."

"He's carrying the don's cigar case," I said.

For a few seconds, we heard only the wind. Javier swallowed and shoved the nickel-framed case out of sight. Miller stared at him coldly. Senator Curtis closed the door and hid inside. Noble Ward recovered long enough to ask, "By what authority do you serve these warrants?"

I handed him the third document, raised my voice so everyone could hear:

"That's my appointment as acting United States marshal for the territory of New Mexico," I said, "pending confirmation by the Senate. It's signed by Former Governor Wallace, Acting Governor Ritch and Wayne MacVeagh, attorney general of the United States of America."

I had no need of free hands anymore. Ten handed me the shotgun. I pressed the stock against my right thigh, fingers in trigger guard, the double barrels trained on Levi Miller.

Ward's face turned pale.

"There's no warrant for you, Ward," I added, hoping that might take him—and his men—out of the fight. "And I think you're too smart to kill a U.S. marshal and his deputy, no matter how many senators you have for a witness."

The door opened again, briefly revealing the blond curls. "Papa?"

"Get inside!" the rancher said. The door shut again. Ward stepped back, raising his hands slightly. "I'm not armed," he pleaded. "I want no part of this. If you want to arrest these men, we won't interfere."

Evaristo spit out his cigar. "You ordered it, Noble Ward!" he said. "And I did not kill the don. Captain Miller did!"

I had never let Miller out of my sight. He grinned. "You got a warrant for me, Mackinnon?"

I let go of the shotgun just long enough to pull his

badge from my outside pocket and toss it at his feet. He laughed.

"Well, I ain't hanging for killing some Mex peasant or beating up some gal. I don't care how many acres they stole. And it'll take more than some half-dime hero and a two-bit lunger to take Leviticus Miller in. So serve your warrant, Ranger Jack."

His hands flashed near his revolvers.

Chapter Nineteen

Moving quickly, I braced the stock against my shoulder and fired the right the barrel. You can't miss at that range with a scattergun, yet I did. Miller brought one of his Smith & Wesson's level and popped off a shot as he bolted for the door. The bullet burned my neck. I swung the shotgun after Miller. Something cracked behind me. Adobe burst above Miller's hat. Tenedore chambered another shell into the Winchester. Miller fired again, tearing off my holster and a chunk of my pants leg and flesh. My finger tightened on the trigger, but Miller disappeared in a shower of glass. Ten's Winchester barked, but Miller was safe, diving through the large window to Noble Ward's office.

Inside the house came two muffled screams. The Smith & Wesson popped once more. A groan. Another shriek. A door slamming.

"Mollie!" A fusillade of gunfire drowned out Ward's cry.

The next thing I realized, I lay facedown on the steps

to the main house, still clutching my shotgun, staring at the blood pooling underneath me. Somehow, I rolled over. A bullet splintered the front door. Another ricocheted nearby. Ten fell beside me, swore, rolled onto his back and shot the rifle from a prone position. One of Ward's hired men grunted.

Keough pitched the Winchester aside and whipped out his Lightning. The Colt fired three times before Ten looked down at me, shoved the revolver in his holster and opened my coat. I didn't like the look on his face.

A rifle slug had slammed into my back just below the ribcage and blown a hole through my shirt front double the size of the entry wound. I couldn't feel anything—the pain would explode later—couldn't even think. Ten swore, said something about getting me out of here and grabbed the collar of my coat. Another round from the bunkhouse took off Ten's Stetson, but he didn't flinch.

Suddenly I caught a movement to my right, saw Javier Evaristo charging, machete in hand. I turned the shotgun slightly and pulled the second trigger. The one-eyed hangman fell as if someone had roped his feet and pulled hard. He hit the ground howling, writhing on the ground and clutching his mangled legs.

Ten spun around, too, but the opposite direction, jerked the Colt and fired. Noble Ward groaned as he fell against the wall and slid down, staining the adobe with his blood. His Remington over-and-under derringer clattered on the porch.

Lead pounded around us. This time Ten winced, ground his teeth and pulled me across the yard to the well about twenty yards from the main house. He ducked as a bullet ripped apart the oaken bucket.

Ten stuck a handkerchief against the exit wound and pressed my left hand against the blood-soaked cloth. Next, he pulled out my Colt and put it in my right hand. The revolver felt like an anvil. I had to rest it on my thigh. "Keep your eyes on that house, Ranger Jack," he said, pausing until the next round of rifle fire ceased. "I'll take care of them bunkhouse boys, but now you gotta watch my back."

I wanted to say, "You did a lousy job watching my back this time," but couldn't manage the words.

Ten ejected the spent cartridges and reloaded the Lightning, ripped off a strip of cotton from his shirt and wrapped it around his left calf, which was leaking blood into his boots.

"I'll get you out of here, amigo," he said, and turned to face the bunkhouse again.

A dozen or more shots cut through the dust and wind. Ten swore, fired twice, cursed again.

"I thought you said those boys would quit," Ten said, "wouldn't fire at a U.S. marshal."

I swallowed and somehow managed to croak out, "My mistake."

Ten laughed, aimed and fired. A yelp told me his slug struck home. Bullets pounded the covering over the well, whined off the rocks, dug up the ground around us like a three-wheeled sulky plow. Ten's Lightning answered. Fighting for breath, he sank beside me to reload, saying: "If they flank us, we're dead."

I figured we were dead anyway.

The front door swung open. I tried to raise my Colt. Ten heard the noise, turned, leveled the .38. Something cracked above us. Ten dived, rolled once, raised his revolver and fired. A man cried out and pitched forward off the roof, crashing to the ground in a crumpled heap with a Spencer repeater falling on his dead face. By the time Ten turned back to the door, he was too late. I saw the muzzle flash, heard Ten groan. I pulled the trigger, didn't come close to the door. As I tried to pull back the hammer, I glanced at Ten. He lay unmoving, his shirt stained red, Lightning on the ground beside his curled fingers.

Levi Miller showed his smiling face. He held Mollie Ward in front of him, his left arm locked around her waist, a Smith & Wesson in his right hand pressed against her blue dress. Tears cascaded down her face and her lips trembled as the Captain forced her outside.

"Hold your fire!" Miller shouted, and the gunmen obeyed.

His spurs jingled as he stepped farther onto the porch. The wind moaned, mingled with the cries of the wounded and dying. I struggled with the Colt, but the hammer felt as if it were rusted shut. Miller glanced at Ten, then me.

"Miller! Let her be."

Miller considered Noble Ward for a second, ignored him and forced Mollie down the steps. He wasn't taking any chances. Finally, he stood over me, keeping Mollie as his shield, and kicked the Colt from my weak hand. Licking his lips, he lowered the barrel of his revolver.

He staggered from the bullet's impact, shoved Mollie on top of me, spun around and fired twice. Mollie screamed, rolled off me and crawled blindly until reaching the dead Tan Ten had shot off the roof. She yelled again, fell backward and saw the bloody trail left by

Javier Evaristo as he drug himself away. Her eyes finally fell on her father, and she just sobbed.

Noble Ward had grabbed his derringer and put a .41-caliber slug into the small of Miller's back. Miller had responded with two shots, one in the rancher's forehead, the other in his heart. Ward sat against the wall, eyes open, derringer still in his right hand. Miller turned to me again, took a step forward, then flew backward onto the porch, slammed against the wall on the other side of Ward and slid down, a giant hole just underneath his center button.

I heard the echo of the shot. For a second, all fell quiet.

"*¡Vamanos!*" a voice shouted. Hoofbeats followed. The war started again. "*¡Viva Don Valentín! ¡Viva Bolivar Viento!*" The crack of guns, curses of men, wails of horses. Teodoro had arrived with his vaqueros, ready for revenge.

Reports came out in the press that Teodoro Valentín rode to the Crown ranch, after burning the Crown Mercantile in Zavala, with three hundred and fifty hardened warriors, and they shot down the gunmen, outnumbered twenty-to-one, like dogs. Teodoro didn't have more than thirty riders, but he had enough.

I tried to pull myself up, but couldn't. Mollie still sat sniffing. Leviticus Miller stared at me, but the light in those cold eyes began to fade. Blood trickled from the corner of his mouth into his gray beard.

"See you in the fires below," he said, and coughed.

"Not likely," I replied.

Finding a last burst of strength, he pulled out his second revolver with his right hand, cocked the hammer and leaned forward on his left hand, trying to steady the Smith & Wesson. His arm gave way, and Miller crumpled onto the porch floor, the revolver toppling end over end down the steps.

Miller spit out a bloody froth. "I hate your miserable guts, Ranger Jack," he said, and died as he had lived.

I struggled for breath as the pain hit, clenching my fists, staring at the dusty sky. The shots died down, replaced by angry Spanish I couldn't understand. Mollie somehow recovered enough to crawl onto the porch beside her father.

"Papa." Her childlike voice still haunts me. "Papa. Wake up, Papa. Please, Papa. Wake up."

Was it worth it? I wondered, figuring to have my answer in a few minutes, delivered by Saint Peter.

My next memory is again of voices. "Teodoro!" I opened my eyes, saw only the sky. The vaqueros had not yet discovered Ten and me, but when I heard the piercing cry, I realized they had found Javier Evaristo. The hangman hadn't crawled fast enough, and when the don's riders found the cigar case, they kicked and clawed at the one-eyed bandit and carried him to the barn.

"No!" Evaristo broke into sobs. "*Por favor. Merced. Merced.* I do not want to die! Nooooo!"

They hanged him inside the barn. Even if I had been able to move, I don't think I could have stopped the mob.

"Amigo."

I looked into Ten's face as he pulled himself into a seated position, resting his back against the well, and cradled my head in his lap. He tried to call out to Teodoro and his men, but they were too busy with their lynching. Ten's face had turned paler than usual, his shirt and trousers soaked with blood, but he managed to smile. I closed my eyes.

"No, Jack. Stay awake. You got to stay awake."

He figured if I went to sleep, I wouldn't wake up. Maybe he was right. But my eyelids turned to stone. He pinched my cheek, but I was hurting enough by then. "Come on, Jack. Tell me a story."

My head shook.

Ten smiled. He called out again for Teodoro, but his voice couldn't carry in the wind. Sighing, he looked down at me. "Then I'll tell you one. Stay awake."

Mollie began to sob again. I tried to block out her voice, concentrate on Tenedore Keough, stay conscious.

"There was once this boy in Charleston, South Carolina," Ten began. "Spoiled rotten by his mama, but he could never do anything right in the eyes of his judge daddy. The boy was fifteen when we fired on Fort Sumter, but Mama didn't want him to enlist in the Army. When conscription came, she talked Daddy into buying a replacement for her only child. The judge hated it, but did it anyway, and went off himself to fight only to lose both legs at Franklin. He came back a bitter old man, looked twenty years older, and loathed his worthless son.

"The boy was worthless, too. After the War, all he did was get into trouble. He broke his poor mother's heart. I don't know, Jack. Maybe he was just trying to make everyone hate him. Maybe he despised himself for his cowardice, for not fighting the Yankees, despised himself for how he treated his parents. Then one night in a saloon, he tangled with some Reconstruction troopers, busted a few heads open and ran home. Mama was furious—first time he'd ever seen her angry—but Daddy said, 'I guess I'll live to see you hang after all.' That scared Mama, and she pleaded for her husband to send the son away. He agreed, but there was a catch. So off went the only child to Baltimore to learn to be a dentist. Uh-uh. Keep your eyes open, amigo.

"He got his degree and came home, found his father but not his mother. 'She's dead,' Daddy says. 'She died six weeks after you left. You broke her heart, Charles Dennis. You killed your poor mother!' The son was enraged. He started choking the old cripple. 'Why didn't you tell me?' he cried. 'Why didn't you let me know so I could come home for the funeral?' Daddy just laughed. 'It was your mother's idea,' he answered. 'She knew if you came back, you wouldn't go back to school, you'd hang after all.' The boy slapped his father, but Daddy kept laughing. 'Didn't you think it strange your mother never wrote you? I guess not. Or you would have written your mother *just once!*' The son just stared at the cripple. 'Get out of this house!' the old man raged.

"So the dentist went west to Birmingham, Alabama, but he spent more time gambling than pulling teeth, consorting with loose women, getting into brawls, trying to kill himself, I guess. He didn't have any friends. Never did. And when he started coughing, when the doctor told him it was consumption, he figured it was God's justice. So he drifted, to Dallas, which was the end of the track then, and hung his shingle again. Only he still spent more time at faro layouts than in his office. No, Jack. Don't go to sleep. I haven't finished.

"And one day, he tried to pull a stranger's tooth. He couldn't do it. The lungs turned on him again. So he tried to provoke his patient into killing him, pulled a gun on the gent, only to break into another deathly cough. But instead of leaving him on the floor, where he belonged, the man helped the pathetic dentist. A few months later, the dentist saw this man again. The dentist pitched in on the stranger's side in a gunfight. Jack? Are you listening to me? That's better.

"Anyway, the dentist knew then he had found a friend.

"Why? He certainly didn't deserve one. He didn't deserve anything good, not the woman who loved him, not the stories and lies and legends written about him, certainly not the fame and money, certainly not an amigo like John L. Mackinnon. He tried hard to make people hate him, but John Mackinnon never did. John Mackinnon made Charles Dennis Tenedore Keough realize he was a man after all."

Ten reached up, wiped his eyes, smiled. "Don't you die on me, Ranger Jack," he whispered.

The world turned black.

Chapter Twenty

In her last Tenedore Keough–Ranger Jack feature, *Rio Diablo Bloodbath; or Ten Keough on the Santa Fe Trail*, Robin K. Hunter wrote that *"cradling Ranger Jack in his arms, Ten willed his trusty companion back to life."* Now, Robin never was one to play straight with the facts—for one thing, the Devil's River is in South Texas, not New Mexico—but I believe Ten did keep me alive.

I have to give some credit to other folks, though: Teodoro and the *vaqueros* who brought me safely back to the *rancho*; Delfina, who came out of bed in spite of her own injuries and seldom left my side; even that old tonsorial artist-turned-sawbones Lando Garcia; and the pair of surgeons from Chicago the Wide Awake Library paid to send down (I suspect Robin had a lot to do with that) to give Ranger Jack the best medical care available. But if not for Charles Dennis Tenedore Keough, I would have croaked in front of the late Noble Ward's home.

VIOLENCE IN SANTA FE COUNTY!
17 LIVES LOST
IN LAND GRANT WAR
RANCHER WARD, SENATOR CURTIS DEAD!
U.S. MARSHAL MORTALLY WOUNDED
DETAILS OF BATTLE

"Mortally wounded." I guess I can't blame the *Santa Fe New Mexican* for printing that headline, or the other publications that picked up the story coast to coast. A newspaper in Richmond, Virginia, wrote that I was dead, causing a stampede of ticket-buyers for Robin's play, *Best of the Bordermen.* And *Frank Leslie's Illustrated* showed a drawing of the vaqueros bowing their heads, crossing themselves, standing in reverent silence over the bodies of Ten Keough and Ranger Jack (Teodoro says this is gospel) and said that I wouldn't survive my wounds. *"His death will mark a sad end to the bitter Valentín Land Grant War, but let us not forget that Ranger Jack Mackinnon died a hero. Let his name be added alongside Crockett's, Travis's, Austin's and Houston's on the Roll of Texas Glory,"* the *Fort Worth Daily Democrat* eulogized.

I fooled 'em all.

But the range war didn't really end with the deaths of Miller, Ward and near-death of me. First, the newspapers demanded justice and an official inquiry when Senator Curtis's body was discovered inside Ward's office. Mollie Ward testified at the inquest that the senator had been hiding behind the desk when Miller jumped through the window. When Curtis leaped up and yelled, Miller shot him in the chest. Mollie ran to her bedroom and locked the door, but Miller kicked it open and grabbed her when she tried to bolt past him.

Mollie found a lawyer in Albuquerque and filed suit against me and a score of other officials, but dropped the matter when the inquest resulted in a finding that cleared me of any wrongdoing. By then, Judge Pike had made public statements that Noble Ward had threatened him, and produced documents linking the rancher to the don's murder. Pike stepped down from the bench, rather than wait to be kicked off, and lit out for Colorado, only to be gunned down by one of Ward's killers near Raton Pass. Meanwhile, the county sheriff, pressured by Ward's friends and gunmen, got warrants charging me and Teodoro with Ward's death, but when he tried to serve him, Delfina forgot that she was the peacekeeper and chased him off with a butcher knife. When the sheriff died—of a heart attack, I might add—two weeks later, a lot of people cried all sorts of things: that he had been poisoned, that Delfina was a witch, that the range war was far from over.

They were right about that. About a dozen or so of Ward's men had escaped from Teodoro's raiders, and a few refused to believe that the deaths of Miller and Ward ended anything. One of those men killed Judge Pike. Another killed two sheepherders on the grant and butchered more than two hundred rams and ewes. All the while, Acting Governor Ritch stewed.

He replaced me with another marshal since I remained "mortally wounded," appointed a temporary county sheriff and waited for Lionel Sheldon of Ohio to take over as territorial governor or the president to declare martial law. And then two things happened unrelated to the Valentín Land Grant War:

On July 2, President James Garfield was assassinated (he died eleven weeks later).

On July 14, Pat Garrett killed Billy the Kid, effectively ending the Lincoln County conflict.

Those two events pushed the Valentín war out of the news, and the violence faded away. Peace came to the land grant. When Governor Sheldon took over, he issued "a proclamation of amnesty for all parties involved in the late Valentín Land Grant War provided they live within the letter of the law or leave the territory at once."

The last of Noble Ward's riders vamoosed. Reporters hounded Mollie Ward for a year or so. Finally, she told a man from *The New York Times*: "Look, my father is dead, Don Valentín is dead. So are the men who killed them. Nothing will bring them back. Please, let me get on with my life." That was in 1883. The last I heard, she had married and was living quietly in Oregon.

I opened my eyes to see the Virgin Mary, her face radiating white and love. It took a while for me to comprehend that the vision before me was a painting, that I was resting in a four-poster bed in Delfina's chambers. She squeezed my hand. I licked my lips, turned on the pillow and saw her. Delfina hadn't slept in days, her face still bruised and lips swollen from Miller's beating, but she looked like an angel.

"Buenas tardes," she said and smiled.

My head cleared slightly. "Ten?" I asked weakly, though I had to say his name twice before she understood.

"You rest, Ranger Jack. You have a long way to go."

My eyes closed. I drifted off the sleep, believing Tenedore Keough had willed me back to life, somehow transferring his will to live into me only to die himself.

I should have known better.

Ten had been shot in the chest and leg, and with his weak lungs, no one expected him to live a week. The question seemed to be who would die first, Ten or me?

I heard the yelp, the shattering of glass, the slamming of a door and angry footsteps getting closer. Delfina, completely healed by now, burst through the door and made a bee line toward me, firing off Spanish that turned my ears red.

"That friend of yours, Ranger Jack! He is . . . *el Diablo*. I will not tend to him anymore." She folded her arms and fell silent.

"What's he doing?"

"His hands! He cannot control his hands. I find it hard to believe he is a friend of yours. I should throw him out of *mi casa*." She went into another tirade before I managed to get in a few words.

"You tell, Mr. Keough," I said, "that if he touches you again, I'll break his hands, one bone at a time."

Delfina smiled. "You cannot get out of bed, Ranger Jack. You cannot break his hands."

"Y'all didn't think I'd be alive now. You had a priest in here reading me my last rites, had an undertaker measuring me for a pine box."

"Mentirosillo," she said, but the smile returned and she sat beside me and gripped my hand.

"Por favor," a heavy voice called from the doorway.

"Allow me to instruct *Señor* Keough on remembering his manners."

Teodoro looked as mean as ever. "Please," I said, "maybe he'll listen to you."

"He'll listen," Meanness said, and for the first time, I saw him smile.

"I won the bet," Ten said, as Lando Garcia wheeled him into my room.

"What bet's that?"

"That I'd get out of bed before you did."

"Who'd you bet?"

"Me."

We shook hands. "Thanks for not dying on me, Ranger Jack."

"Likewise."

Delfina brought in a pitcher of water, kissed me on the cheek, glared at Ten and left the room. Lando filled two glasses, handed me one, but Ten refused and pulled a pewter flask from inside his nightshirt. I shook my head. Ten grinned.

"Your girlfriend calls me troublesome."

Lando grunted. "She calls you much worse, *señor.*"

We laughed and made a toast.

Finally, Ten said quietly, "Robin's in Santa Fe."

His eyes reflected inward. I stared at my glass of water. Lando quietly left the room, closing the door behind him. Ten looked at me.

"You should go see her," I said.

His head bobbed. "She sent word that she's staying at the Exchange. Didn't want to ride out here, see us all shot up. You know how she is. I think . . ."

"Go to her, amigo," I said. "You deserve her. You both deserve to be happy."

"I can't make anyone happy."

"You can try."

He took another pull on his flask. "Maybe," he said, smiled, tried to change the subject. "Lando tells me people are still talking you up for county sheriff. Says even if you don't run, they'll write you in on the ballots."

"Go to Robin, Ten," I said.

"Then who would watch your back?"

"Go."

He returned his flask and called out for Lando. As Garcia wheeled him out the door, Ten put his hand on the door frame, turned and said, "Take care of yourself, John Mackinnon."

"Watch your back," I told him.

Part Four, Glenwood Springs, Colorado
Sunday, July 8, 1883

Chapter Twenty-One

The scent of pine was strong outside the rectangular building on a hilltop overlooking the town. A lot of consumptives came to Glenwood Springs for the sulfur vapors, and when the springs failed, they moved into the Saint Jude Sanatorium of Western Colorado to die. All around town, I heard the bustle of tourists and shouts of children at play, everyone enjoying a wonderful summer afternoon. Rich forests, glorious mountains and beautiful homes dominated Glenwood Springs. I didn't want to go inside the sanatorium, didn't want to see what I knew I had to face.

Delfina and I had tried to talk Ten into staying with us after the range war, but he remarked that he had places to see and faro games to deal. He had seen Robin in Santa Fe, and I knew he would head east to her. Ten shook my hand, left the territory and rode out of my life. "You get into a jam, Ranger Jack, just let me know," he said. "After all, someone's got to watch your back."

I didn't get into any jams, even though I served two

years as sheriff of Santa Fe County. "The Lawman Without A Gun," one dime novel called me. But I didn't need a gun. Not anymore. After retiring as a lawman, I stayed on with Delfina and Teodoro, learning to be a rancher and cowboy while earning a little extra cash as a part-time gunsmith. We heard about Ten, though, through the papers and the cheap novels found at the mercantile. He married Robin Hunter in September of '81, and she took him on a lecture tour—*True Stories from the Frontier; an Evening with Tenedore Keough*—across the Northeast while churning out several more works for the Wide Awake Library featuring new heroes, not Ten and me. The big cities didn't do Ten's lungs any good, and his fights with Robin also became newsworthy, especially when she had him arrested on New Year's Day, 1883. Finally, Ten left Robin, or maybe she threw him out, a few weeks later. Some say he was a hardcase who treated his loving wife poorly. I think he did it because he didn't want her to see him suffer and die. Robin never wrote me, and the last news about Ten came that spring when a horse buyer told me Ten had been herding sheep in Colorado before selling his herd and moving to Leadville, back to the faro layouts.

Then I got the telegram, and here I stood.

Ten had drifted to Glenwood Springs for the sulfur treatment, but his consumption had been too widespread, and the fumes destroyed what little lungs he had left. I took off my hat, opened the door and went inside. I told a nun my name, and followed her down a dark hall to the last room on the left, the echoes of my boots unnerving me even more. She showed me inside, shut the door behind me.

Ten had wasted away to sallow skin pulled taut over brittle bones. His breathing was short and ragged, his eyes sunk deep in his head. Trembling hands held a deck of cards, and a bottle of rye, flanked by two empty shot glasses and a tumbler of water, stood on the table by his bedside. He stopped his game of solitaire, smiled and motioned me to a nearby chair.

"Been a while, pard." I had to strain to hear his words. I reached over and clasped his frail hands. "Welcome to the death watch," he said.

Shaking my head and forcing a smile, I said, "You'll bury us all, Keough."

His eyes glinted. "I'll take that bet, Ranger Jack."

I waited in silence, aware of my own breathing and Ten's strains for life.

"Ain't the way I figured to go," he finally whispered. "No bullet, huh? I'm glad you come, Jack. Didn't want to die alone. You'll see that Robin gets my belongings. Tell her . . ."

"I'll tell her," I said.

"You ever marry that Mexican gal?"

"Delfina? No, not yet."

"What are you waiting for?"

"I'm stupid. You know that."

"Don't wait too long, Jack." He nodded, licked his lips and caught his breath. "You marry her, name the first boy after me. She's a good woman. So's Robin. . . ."

We didn't say anything for a few minutes, just stared at each other. He went through a wicked coughing spell that brought two nuns inside, but finally controlled his breathing and waved his hands at the women.

"These sisters," he said, smiling again, "have converted me, Jack, saved my soul, even had Father Pasquale read me the last rites. Sister Madeleine over there, I don't think she expected me to stick around for your arrival. She don't know me."

He coughed once, swallowed and said, "You're my only friend, Jack Mackinnon. I'll always be there for you, 'cause you were always there for me."

I bowed my head, felt the tears stream down my face, squeezed his hand gently and choked out, "Ten . . ."

That's all I could say. I wanted to tell him how much I owed him, how much I loved him, tell him that through it all, he was the best friend I ever had. He let my pain run its course, and when I looked up and wiped my face, his eyes held that mischievous glint I had seen so many times.

"Don't you go counting Ten out just yet, Ranger Jack. Somebody's got to watch your back."

After I tried to laugh, Ten nodded at the rye. "How about a drink, old friend?"

My head motioned to the two nuns I knew stood behind me. "Don't worry about them, Jack," he said. "Sister Madeleine's deeply in love with me, and Sister Ruth bought the bottle herself."

I rose and filled the two shot glasses, placed one on his chest and waited until he gripped the glass with icy fingers. I made a toast and took a sip. Ten didn't move.

"Jack," he said, "I can't lift a full glass of rye. Ain't that the funniest thing you ever heard. . . ." He started to laugh, but never finished.

Clenching my teeth to keep from crying again, I placed my glass on the table, picked up Ten's, closed his eyes and stepped away. Sister Ruth, citing a soft prayer, covered Ten's face with the bedsheet, while tears rolled down Sister Madeleine's cheeks. "I'll leave you alone," she said, and the two nuns hurried out of the room.

I don't know how long I stood there. An hour, I think. Just standing, crying, remembering. I heard a man clear his throat and turned. A priest put his hand on my shoulder, told me that Charles Dennis Tenedore Keough stood with the Lord now, no consumption, no pain. Then he handed me my rye, picked up Ten's untouched drink and raised the glass.

"To Ten Keough," he said.

Our glasses clinked together. I glanced at the body, smiled and said, "Here's how, Ten."

The priest and I downed the rye.

Epilogue

Sunday, May 16, 1886
New Mexico Territory

In the end, Ten and me both found what we were looking for: peace, at last, and a place to be. The reporters polished off my whiskey about the time a boy knocked on the door. Teodoro's son Vasco was cute as a button in that little black suit, the spitting image of old Don Valentín.

"They are ready, *patrón*," Vasco said timidly, afraid of the strangers inside. One of the reporters, who had too much of my free liquor, slapped my back and said, "Don't keep the lady waiting, Ranger Jack."

Laughing, the other reporters followed him out the door to take their places outside.

"*¿Patrón?*" Vasco said, holding the door open.

"I'll be there in a minute, Vasco," I said. "Just let me straighten my tie."

He smiled and walked away, leaving me alone with my thoughts. It was my wedding day, but for a few moments, I felt sad. Delfina was a wonderful woman, that's for sure, but right now I missed Ten. I missed him a lot, wished his marriage with Robin would have worked out, wished he could have been here, hoped he knew how much I really loved him. I straightened my tie, brushed the dust off my suit and walked outside.

New Mexico's beautiful this time of year, and we had a glorious day, a cloudless blue sky and no wind, the mountains shining all around our place. My nerves fell apart again. It looked like all of Santa Fe and half of the territory stood outside, spilling out of the tiny chapel, lining the *placita,* granary, even sitting on the walls. I recognized a few smiling faces, smelled the brisket smoking for our reception. A vaquero motioned for me to hurry up and take my place so Delfina could begin her march. I took a tentative step forward, glanced up the hill overlooking the *rancho.*

The fence had been painted white this spring, and flowers bloomed around it. I couldn't see the marble Celtic cross, but I knew it was there, knew the words by heart:

CHARLES DENNIS TENEDORE KEOUGH

DENTIST & FRIEND

1846–1883

I relaxed and walked toward the priest. Ten wasn't gone. He said he would always be there for me, and I knew he hadn't lied. From his perch on the hill, he'd have a good view of the wedding today. In years to come, he'd see my children christened and grow to adulthood. And he would be there, as always, to watch my back.